Threshold

CATHY M. DOYLE

All the best

[signature]

Produced by:

FriesenPress
Suite 300 – 852 Fort Street
Victoria, BC, Canada V8W 1H8

www.friesenpress.com

Distributed to the trade by The Ingram Book Company

For Chelsey

A Note from the Author

I want to thank everybody who has supported me and encouraged me to put this book into print. If I attempted to name people, I would leave too many out. It took three years to complete and another two to send it to the printers. I do need to thank Robert Wiseman at Gotit-Needit-Wantit Musical Instruments, Courtenay, BC for supplying the percussion instruments for the cover art and Lori for the inspiration she gave me. I also would not have completed this without the support of Glenn, Wanda and Brian.

This entire story; characters and scenarios, are purely fiction and completely from my imagination. There is no person or event that this is based upon.

Despite this story being a work of fiction, addictions and situations of abuse are very real. If you or someone you know needs help, please do not hesitate to seek professionals in your area. You do not ever have to suffer in silence or alone.

God Bless you.

Chapter One

It was early autumn in Chicago, Illinois. The sun still shone intensely and hot during the day but the shade and nights were becoming chilly. In the city core, buildings crowded each other as busy people passed by every day. Each person had their own agendas, thoughts and business to attend to. They also had their own unique set of circumstances, problems and dreams.

One of these buildings contained a company, only identified by its name on a list near the elevator. It was small but spread over several floors. Within this unassuming business, many deals were struck, many lives were changed and thousands were entertained.

Currently, a small group of men sat in a large conference room. Their leader paced to and fro in front of them, sipping his fifth coffee of the day. Benjamin Dapril was a very popular and successful music-recording producer. He started out as a young singer/songwriter and after twenty years as a semi-successful artist, he turned his attention and talents to producing and promoting others. He worked with recording companies for seven years and then decided to go out on his own. He developed Benjamin Dapril Independent Productions. Soon after, his company became known as B.D.I. Productions, which spoken quickly turned out to be quite humorous. He then officially renamed his company Beady Eye Productions.

Now as a fifty-four year old, grey haired and slightly overweight producer/promoter, Benjamin and his company had been handling many acts for over twenty years. They had many small names that were not very successful and a few that enjoyed great success. On these few, Benjamin spared no expense or effort in doing whatever it took to aid in the continued success of these acts. One such act was a band called Threshold.

Threshold had been together for over three years with no changes in their members. Their current line-up was a five-member group. Michael Mitchell was the male lead singer and keyboard player. Rex Landers was the guitar player who sang back-up vocals. Peter Louring was a young but talented bass player with a nice supporting voice. Andy Zellers was the oldest and most experienced member who not only was a very talented drummer but also handled the band's finances as well as worked as an accountant for Beady Eye. The fifth member was the female lead vocalist named Theresa MacKenzie. She had worked with

Mike on other projects and they decided together with Rex to put Threshold together, adding the other members after.

Threshold released their latest recording project six months earlier. This CD was entitled "Multiple Sides" and was selling well. With two singles on the charts, a music video was in the editing stages, Threshold was becoming very popular, especially in their home area of Chicago. Demands for live performances were pouring in.

Benjamin knew most of these players well and foresaw from the beginning a problem with Theresa. He knew that Theresa had given up the live scene years earlier and had worked as a session vocalist in the studio. He felt that in joining Threshold, she would eventually get tired and want to move on. Even though she performed in the live shows and took part in the production of the video for "Dancing Angel", she did start to tire and expressed a desire to take on a simpler life. She joined Threshold to help Mike and to do it for fun, however now that the demand was getting great, she couldn't keep up.

Benjamin had called the remaining four members into Beady Eye's downtown Chicago offices for a meeting. They had gathered in a large but comfortable conference room.

"Guys," began Benjamin, "this CD is selling like hot cakes. Everyday, several more radio stations across the U.S. and in Canada are picking up both singles. "Dancing Angel" is in the top twenty on the charts and "Colorful Wishes" seems to be heading the same way. Your upcoming live shows are selling out because the buying public wants to experience Threshold personally. We're working out deals for some shows across the U.S. and in Canada. I don't think Europe is out of reach and my people in Australia are making waves for you.

"We've developed a problem though. As you can see, Theresa is not here today. I thought that a day would come that we would be having this discussion, and here we are. Theresa is burning out again and needs someone to replace her. We need to find another female vocalist for Threshold. I really don't see any way around the fact. We would need to find one that's just as good and who would be available to give one-hundred percent into the group and into touring."

"What's Theresa going to be doing?" asked Peter.

"Theresa has been a studio session singer for years before she joined Threshold. Work on another recording project is available and she wants to do it. The live shows are just too much for her to handle. She burnt out her vocal chords awhile back and she feels she's heading that way again. She needs to take care of herself before she does any permanent damage. She will continue to fulfill her obligations for upcoming shows until we can find a replacement for her. We will need that to happen soon."

"Got any ideas?" asked Rex.

"I've starting making a few lists. When I have a manageable number, we'll arrange some auditions and on-stage trials. There's a lot of talent out there and if we can snag a girl who's already got an established following, that would be an advantage."

"Just because she's good doesn't mean she'll fit it," said Mike. "Theresa fit it."

Andy laughed. "Acquiring Pete was a lot of fun. We must have auditioned over a hundred bassists and tried out at least thirty on stage before Pete here clicked into place. Mike and Rex are so fussy; they don't know how to accept anything less than perfection."

Peter blushed noticeably. "I thought for sure I screwed up so much that first show that you'd kick me out fast."

Mike replied, "Well, you did make a bunch of mistakes, but that was nerves. We knew the minute we started playing together that your talent and personality would fit in just fine. It's just something we feel."

They discussed some equipment purchases for the live stage shows and the hiring of security and technical staff. Beady Eye Productions had established personnel that worked on a regular basis, but they wanted to hire a few other freelance individuals to take on tour with them. They agreed to try out some new individuals during the auditions and trials for the female vocalist. The meeting ended very upbeat and the men left the office chatting about future dreams and expectations in the months to come.

Mike and Rex were both thirty-five years old. They went to high school together and had been performing both together and separately for the past twenty years. They both had known Theresa for ten years when she easily convinced Rex and Mike to join again musically. They had the same desires and expectations both musically and personally. They were more like brothers than friends.

Mike was the more natural leader of the two. He enjoyed being the center of attention. He was tall at six-feet, four inches and towered over the others on stage. His blonde hair and blue eyes were a magnet for many female fans. Mike was always one to find an excuse for a party, to tell jokes and have a good time.

Mike's wife, Cora, was also thirty-five. She was a full foot shorter than Mike at only five-feet, four inches. She also had blonde hair but her eyes were a sparkling green. Cora was quiet by nature and worked as a nurse in various hospitals around the Chicago area. Because of the diversity of their careers, they decided not to have children, but their twelve-year marriage was very strong.

Cora always remained happy and positive, despite the difficulties in Mike's career. She was a very confident and observant woman who worked hard in her career as well as the wife of a musician. She loved to take care of people and her keen observations often caught small changes in patients and their care. Things were obvious to Cora that others failed to notice. Using these talents, she was a wonderful nurse and a wonderful wife. She could see the thrill and excitement in her husband's life as he finally fulfilled his dreams. She was happy that he would be as successful in his career as she was in hers.

Rex was shorter and quieter. He was five-feet, ten inches and in great physical shape. There was a time when he wouldn't turn down a good party. He lived that lifestyle for years, but slowed down after he saw it become personally destructive. He would now prefer to exercise or jog instead of party. He also held a black belt in Karate. He was very muscular with a dark complexion, deep brown eyes and thick brown hair. He was married to Mike's younger sister, Pam.

She also had blonde hair and blue eyes like her brother and was also five-feet, ten inches. They complemented each other and were a very nice looking couple.

When Rex and Pam decided to marry ten years earlier, Mike was thrilled. Their families encouraged their relationship and had their wedding planned very early in their relationship. Mike and their parents married them in a very flamboyant celebration.

Pam was thirty-two years old and as Mike's younger sister, knew a lot about the music industry. She was also a very talented singer and performed as a teenager with Mike and Rex in their bands. After high school, however, she was not comfortable with living the lifestyle of a performer. She left their young band and attended university to obtain a degree in Interior Design. She had a natural flair for design and enjoyed the more stable career choice with a regular income.

With her intimate knowledge of the industry, Pam realized very early in her relationship with Rex they could not depend upon his income. Months would go by that only her income supported them. Often she worried about her husband's chosen profession and the financial burden that fell upon her shoulders. In the early years, she always worked extra hard to bring in money but fell short too often. Things were a little more comfortable, but the fear was always there, so she had been creating her own savings in case of hard times again.

Andy was forty-two years old and he had been involved in the music scene for twenty-seven years. Balding brown hair with grey at the edges and glasses made Andy look more like the accountant than the musician. He kept the book-keeping up to date and made certain finances were running smoothly for all of Beady Eye's bands. He worked out expenses, allowances, payments and budgets for all the individuals in each band.

Andy approached large corporations for sponsorship of tours. Whether it was displaying a logo, wearing certain clothes or footwear, or even eating or drinking a certain product, the bands went along with whatever Andy suggested. It meant money was coming in to pay for the many expenses that went along with touring like accommodations, booking concert halls, paying everyone involved as well as food and travel.

Andy lived alone since his bitter divorce five years earlier. He had worked with Mike on various projects over the past fifteen years and he felt honored when Mike asked him to help him set up Threshold. He was also grateful for the work and the distraction from his personal problems. Becoming their drummer was just a fun way to save the band a bit of money by not having to pay for a separate bookkeeper. He got a little extra in payment for his services and he was satisfied with that.

Andy joined the band shortly after Rex did and bass players came and went. The original four got along very well. A trust and respect bonded them together. Theresa, Mike, Rex and 'Old Man Andy' not only became good friends, they became the Threshold family. Any member joining had to be accepted into the 'family' and all four immediately knew it if the new member would work or not.

Peter was only twenty-six and aside from garage bands in high school and cover bands in college, this was his first professional band. He was slender and six feet tall with red hair, brown eyes and freckles that made him look like a kid. Finding him was a highlight of Threshold's history. This fifth member had been difficult to find, but Peter fit in from the beginning.

Peter's young wife was only twenty years old. Cindy was very familiar with the financial struggles of life in the music industry. She and Peter had been married for two years and they had a three-year old son named Kevin. Kevin was a high-energy child with Peter's red hair and freckles. Not being able to afford any kind of daycare program, Cindy worked during the daytime as a teacher's aid while Peter looked after their son and played evenings and weekends. She was not happy about Peter joining Threshold because of the time away from home it required of him. Cindy knew that she would soon have to quit her job while he was away thus adding to their financial difficulties.

Cindy never felt like she fit in with the Threshold Family. She was much younger than the other wives were and she was the only one with a child. Cora and Pam had a long family connection history and had a lot in common. Nevertheless, Cindy was included in everything that was going on and everyone tried to make her feel welcome. They made it clear that once someone was involved with Threshold on a regular basis, this family adopted them regardless of circumstances.

Pam and Cora often babysat for Cindy when she needed to run errands or to just get away alone for a while. They were good friends and she felt lucky to have such a supportive family keeping her safe and involved. They bought Kevin a backyard swing set and had their yard fenced in as an early Christmas present. Peter and Cindy rented the house that they were living in, but Peter hoped that he would earn a good living with Threshold and be able to buy a proper house for his family one day.

Threshold began looking for a replacement for Theresa. It was proving difficult to find another Threshold family member personality that fit in with them. There was a lot of talent out there, but it often came with attitude and vanity problems. They were looking for someone that would gladly share the spotlight, not steal it. The ones whose personality fit it were not very good singers or had a poor on-stage presence. No one had yet clicked into place and the guys were holding out for the perfect fit.

The remaining four band members and Benjamin could not agree on any one girl in particular. After many auditions, they narrowed the list down to four possibilities. Beginning the next week, they would try them out on stage once again and try to decide whether to accept one of these women. They all agreed that the perfect fifth member was out there, they just have not found her yet.

Chapter Two

Pam Landers worked for a very busy interior design firm called Home Comforts. She was one of four staff interior decorators, but she was the busiest and most requested. Each employee represented the firm, but worked with their own clients. For the past year, Pam felt that she had a strong client base and was considering going out on her own. She had already registered herself as an independent company and was going to call her company Mitchell-Landers Designs. Her ongoing fear of financial stability kept her back. She just needed that one good break.

Pam had gotten a phone call from a young professional couple who were in the process of building a new home and wanted to have it decorated professionally. Mr. and Mrs. Baker had arranged an initial meeting with Pam to get to know one another and discuss designs, colors, styles and techniques. They were meeting Wednesday evening at seven o'clock at a popular nightclub called Bobbi-Jo's which was close to the apartment that the couple were currently renting while their house was being built.

Bobbi-Jo's had a reputation for its excellent food and good entertainment. Pam thought it an unlikely place for a meeting because local and visiting musicians get on stage and have an impromptu jam session every Wednesday evening. Often, a wide variety of performers showed up to play and no one ever knew who was going to come or what was going to happen. Pam herself had been on that stage many times both by herself and with Mike and Rex. It was always a lot of fun for the performers and the audience, but it also got loud and confusing. She wasn't certain that it was an ideal location for an initial client meeting, but the clients chose it, so she agreed.

Pam was very excited about this contract. If she was successful with this one, she was finally going to leave Home Comforts and start Mitchell-Landers. The Bakers wanted to decorate the entire house. It was by far her biggest contract yet. She had done renovations to several rooms at once but never designed an entire house from the beginning. She wanted this contract badly and did not want to be late. Rex wasn't home when she left for the meeting so she left a note and decided to fill him in on the details later. He always supported her in her decisions and listened to her ideas, but he admitted honestly to her that he wasn't overly interested in interior design. He was happy with a fresh coat of paint and some furniture but loved to see how excited she got during each new job and talked her through the frustrations that naturally came with them.

Pam met with George and Beverly Baker a few minutes early and they sat at a table near the stage.

"We come here almost every Wednesday," said Beverly. "It's sort of 'date night'. I hope you don't mind too much that we selected this spot."

"Not at all," replied Pam, "I like it here."

By eight o'clock, Pam's meeting with the Bakers was going very well. They were working out schedules, design ideas and finances when the jamming musicians began to come onto the stage. The Bakers agreed to another appointment for Friday evening at Bobbi-Jo's at seven o'clock and invited Pam to join them for the evening for food and drinks. She gladly accepted and even offered to pick up the tab. She wanted to make a good impression and the personal investment was an acceptable expense.

Pam continued to chat with her new clients between songs and changeovers in performers. She was not paying much attention to the stage until suddenly she heard an amazing voice hit the speakers. She turned her attention to the stage to see a very beautiful woman with an incredible voice and an exciting stage presence.

After the woman's song, Bobbi-Jo herself, acting as host for the event, came to the microphone and introduced the on-stage performers. She introduced the incredibly talented woman as The Flower Girl and that she was there every week as a regular performer. Bobbi-Jo also invited anyone else who wanted to come on stage to perform and a few more performers took turns going on stage.

Throughout the next few songs, the various musicians on stage seemed to feed off The Flower Girl's talent and personality. There was something very captivating about her and Pam could feel it as well. She knew that Threshold wanted to replace Theresa and thought that perhaps this young woman might be a good fit. She hesitated, unsure of her feelings and of what to do. Finally, she excused herself from the Bakers and stepped into the washroom. Using her cellular phone, she phoned home, hoping that Rex was there.

"Hello!" Rex answered.

"Hi, it's me. I'm at Bobbi-Jo's. I want you to listen to something."

Pam left the washroom and went back into the club. She held her phone in the air so Rex could hear the woman that was demanding the attention of everyone in the room.

"Can you hear her?" Pam shouted into the phone.

"Don't let her leave!" exclaimed Rex. "I'm on my way!"

Thirty minutes later, Rex arrived at Bobbi-Jo's. He saw Pam sitting at a table alone near the stage. He went over to her, kissed her on the cheek and sat down at her table.

"Where is she?" Rex asked Pam.

Rex looked over at the stage while Pam told him, "I got the contract! I'm going to do the Bakers' entire house, room by room. I'm going to be very busy but it's going to bring in a lot of money."

Rex was still looking at the stage. The musicians were playing an instrumental and there were two women on stage.

"That's nice, dear. Which one is she?"

"She's not there. She's over at the bar getting a drink."

Pam pointed to a tall, beautiful woman wearing jeans and a pink sweater. Her clothes were very simple but looked expensive. She was around five feet, ten inches and had very long straight blonde hair that flowed down to her waist. She was in obvious great physical condition and had a very sexy figure. Her simple attire was not provocative; however, she exhibited sexiness in her confident attitude and posture.

Rex watched her as she took her drink and went back to the stage. Pam was still trying to get Rex's attention.

"With these new clients, I'm thinking of quitting my job."

"That's nice."

"I want to start up Mitchell-Landers as soon as I clear my obligations with Home Comforts. I'm going to go it alone."

"Super."

"The money may not be as regular."

"Yup."

Rex stared at The Flower Girl and wondered at her name when Pam began to get irritated. She knew that this woman was the reason why he was here and she was the one who called him down to check her out, however, she wanted him to listen to her news as well.

"I may have to travel a lot on my own."

"OK."

"Rex, are you even listening to me?"

"Of course I am, Pam." Rex looked at her and took her hand. "Honey, you are very talented at what you do. Money is no longer an issue for us with the success of the band. I have every confidence in you that you will be extremely successful on your own. I support you completely in whatever you decide to do. If you have to travel, just do it safely. The money you bring in will be all yours and not a mere percentage of what Home Comforts gives you for all your efforts and talents. You can easily get a client base just by word of mouth and some advertising. I'll help you in any way that I can. We'll start by renovating that spare room into a proper office. I happen to know of an excellent interior decorator that would be perfect for the job."

Rex laughed and squeezed Pam's hand. She smiled although she felt slightly disappointed. That spare room had originally been set aside for a baby's nursery, but after so many years of marriage, no babies came and although they did not discuss it, they both accepted the fact that they would most likely remain childless. Pam was extremely disappointed and she decided to pursue her career without feelings of guilt. She kept busy to fill the void.

"I've got an early morning," said Pam. "You enjoy the jam. Good luck with talking to this girl. I hope things work out with her."

"I didn't thank you for calling me down. If this turns into something spectacular, you will be responsible for it all!"

Pam smiled weakly and left.

Meanwhile, the musicians had started another song and The Flower Girl played percussion enhancements and sang back-up vocals again. She enhanced every song she participated in with her voice and her percussive sounds. She was extremely talented, just as Pam had said. Her stage presence was undeniably formidable. He could not take his eyes off her. The song finished and they announced that The Flower Girl was going to sing the next song, which was a very powerful ballad. Rex sat up straighter and started unconsciously wringing his hands together. He was very impressed with her so far. He was excited to see her really in action. She sang beautifully. She was pitch-perfect, her range was incredible and her power was immense. The whole package that Threshold was looking for was about twenty feet in front of him. Would she be willing to take on the role?

They performed for another two hours. Rex sat transfixed on this incredible woman on the stage. They performed a wide variety of music and The Flower Girl was impeccable in each style, with each group of artists. When she didn't sing the lead vocals, she continued to impress with her enhancements in vocal backings and percussion.

After the jam session was over, the performers packed up their belongings. Rex went over to the stage and watched The Flower Girl pack away her percussion instruments into a flowered suitcase. As she stepped off the stage, Rex approached her.

"Excuse me. May I please speak with you for a moment?"

The girl had seen Rex sitting at his table. She was aware of his intense scrutiny throughout the evening, which had made her very nervous. Despite this, she was curious about him so she stopped. He looked pleasant and had a gentle voice so she decided to find out what his interest in her was. She was very inebriated and that gave her courage to speak to him.

"What can I do for you?" she asked Rex.

"My name is Rex Landers. I'm here as a representative of the Beady Eye recording artists Threshold. Have you heard of us?"

"Of course. I don't think you can live in Chicago and not hear of Threshold. You're very good."

"Thank you. First of all, may I ask you your name?"

"I'm Lily Rose," she smiled, revealing perfect white teeth. She extended her hand.

Rex shook her hand and returned her smile. "Ah, The Flower Girl. I get it. That's very clever. May we sit for a moment?" He motioned toward a nearby table. As soon as they sat, a server came over.

"Last call," the server informed them. "Would you like anything?"

Rex shook his head. "No thanks."

"I'll have my usual," Lily told her.

The server left and Rex was anxious to pitch his idea to Lily.

"This is going to sound outright crazy. I want you to join Threshold."

"What? You don't even know me!"

"If you're familiar with Threshold's stuff, you'll know that we have a female vocalist. Her name is Theresa MacKenzie and she's moving on to other projects. This is leaving us with a major challenge to replace her with someone extremely talented with a great stage personality that would fit in with the rest of us. I watched you up on that stage all evening and I truly believe that you are the perfect fit!"

The server returned with Rum and Cola and Lily handed her a credit card to pay her tab for the evening. She took her time and took a couple of drinks before answering.

"I don't know what to say. This is not something I'm really looking for in my life at this time. I'm a very private person and don't like a lot of attention. I do this on Wednesdays because it's fun. This is the only place I have ever sang or performed in any way. I have never belonged to a band in my life. I have a couple of part-time jobs plus this gig and that pays my bills."

"You are good enough to be a professional."

"I just do this for fun."

"Surely, you must have been approached with serious offers before."

"I've had quite a few people want me to consider joining them when they find out that I have no other professional commitments. I also have had many other offers that had nothing to do with music. I didn't accept those either."

Lily picked up her drink and finished it quickly. Rex pulled a business card out of his wallet and handed it to her.

"This card is for the recording company we belong to. The main producer's name is Benjamin Dapril. I would appreciate it if you would at least consider auditioning. Could you come to our office around three o'clock Friday afternoon and meet with us? No obligations. Just come by and chat with all of us in an office setting. We can tell you all about us. You can meet us and ask us whatever you want. We'll explain what our plans are and how you can help us achieve our goals. We'll work out what's in it for you. Please think about it."

"I'm really not sure. I'm extremely flattered, but this isn't who I am." She began to giggle. "This whole situation is very surreal for me. You have to admit that this is a bit sudden. And I'm not exactly sober right now either."

"I'm sorry. It's just that I have such a good feeling about this. Just think about it. Come and talk to us on Friday. I promise you that you'll owe us nothing more."

"I'll think about it, but I'm not committing to anything."

"I don't expect you to. Just consider meeting us to start with."

Lily stood up and Rex followed her lead.

"Thank you. This has been…" Lily paused, "…interesting."

She offered him her hand and he took it. Instead of shaking it however, he just held it. He looked into her blue eyes and their beauty transfixed him.

"I have a very good feeling about you, Lily Rose," Rex said. "Please, give it some serious thought."

Lily removed her hand from Rex's and smiled. "I promise to think it over."

Chapter Three

On Friday afternoon at ten minutes before three o'clock, there was a nervous but excited energy in the offices of Beady Eye Productions. Mike, Peter, Andy and Benjamin sat at the conference table. Rex paced nervously in front of the conference room window.

"Would you sit down?" asked Peter. "You're making us all nervous."

"Gee, you'd think Pam was giving birth or something," quipped Andy.

Rex glared at him. "That's not funny. This is important to all of us. She's the one. I can feel it!"

Benjamin stood and walked over to the coffee machine. He poured himself the third cup of coffee that hour. He was upset with Rex. He felt that Rex usurped his authority by discovering an unknown talent and was angry that if this worked out, Rex would get the credit and not he.

"This girl may not even show up," Benjamin grumbled. "You said she didn't sound interested in us. She never called to confirm."

"She didn't call to cancel," countered Rex.

"What exactly do you know about her anyway?" Benjamin asked.

"She has the voice. She has the talent. She has the stage presence. She has everything we've been looking for but haven't found in all the others. Her vocal range is incredible. Her percussion enhancements is something even Theresa doesn't have. She adapted with every performer that got on that stage with her. She's the one!"

"I did as much research as I could," said Mike. "There's no record of Lily Rose anywhere. The only confirmation of her existence is Bobbi-Jo herself. The only thing she could tell me is that she showed up three years ago and has been a regular almost every Wednesday evening. She doesn't even know anything else about her. Lily Rose is a big mystery."

"She's just been doing this for fun and she said she was a very private person."

"We're going to need more than a talented woman," said Benjamin. "We need someone that is willing to commit to the long haul. I have invested too much into Threshold to put someone in who is in it just for kicks. You have all worked too hard to be let down by someone unreliable. You need the best."

"She is the best," Rex insisted.

"Face it, Rex. She's an unknown that struck your fancy on whatever level she struck it. She just may not show up. You have to admit, you might have scared her."

"There's one other thing," added Mike. "This was not a group decision. You were on your own on Wednesday night. We may see things that you didn't."

"You're questioning both me and Pam. Don't forget, Pam found her. I just went to check her out. I was planning to tell you about her the next day. When I was there however, I just knew that I had to act immediately. Wait unit she gets here. You'll all accept her!"

"What makes you so certain that she'll show up?" asked Andy.

"Wouldn't you?" responded Rex. "I would at least show up out of curiosity to see what this offer was all about. There would be no harm in that. I promised her there would be no obligations after this meeting."

At exactly three o'clock, the intercom buzzed. Benjamin, still standing with his coffee, answered his secretary's summons.

"Yes?" Benjamin spoke into the speakerphone.

"There's a lady here to see you and Rex regarding Threshold. Should I bring her in?"

"Yes, Ruth. Thank you." Benjamin turned the speaker off. "For Heaven's sake, Rex, sit down!"

Rex sat but as the door opened and Ruth showed Lily Rose into the room, he stood again. Benjamin went over to greet her and offered her his hand. As Lily took it, he started to shake it, but found himself awkwardly silent. Finally, Lily removed her hand from his.

"Miss Rose. Thank you so much for coming. Rex has told us all about you. Thank you, Ruth."

Ruth left and closed the door behind her. Peter stood up and offered Lily a chair. Benjamin had been a professional for most of his life and dealt with many people over the years. He had never experienced the awkwardness before that he had just felt. Her radiant beauty captivated him and his mind was a blank.

"Please have a seat," Benjamin finally found enough voice to say. "Let me introduce you to the members of Threshold."

Lily sat and smiled as Peter pushed in her chair. Pete blushed slightly and sat down beside her. Rex finally sat and looked relieved but nervous.

Benjamin remained standing to maintain his heir of authority. He offered her a coffee, which she refused, then introduced himself and the rest of the members, telling her what position each one had in the band. He left Rex until last.

"You've already met Rex. He is our guitar player and sings back up as well. He's our representative that we send out to look for new talent."

Rex almost laughed at Benjamin's attempt to maintain superiority. In making it sound as if Rex was acting on Benjamin's orders, Benjamin appeared to be control over everything that happened.

"We really appreciate you coming down today to speak with us, Miss Rose," Benjamin continued.

"Just call me Lily. I couldn't resist. I was very curious at your offer. I never had anyone approach me with an offer this big. I'm very interested in what you have to say. I have to admit that I did quite a bit of research on the Internet. Confident that you are legitimate, I'm here. I'm nervous, but curious."

"Did Rex explain to you what we're looking for?"

"We didn't have a lot of time to chat which is why he asked me to come here. I understand that your female vocalist is moving on to other things and you're hurrying to find a replacement. He thinks that my talents will fill the void that she's leaving."

"We're not in a hurry," Benjamin answered, not wanted to appear desperate. "We've been searching for awhile and actually do have it narrowed down to four choices. Theresa would like us to make a final decision so she can move on and we've appreciated that she has stayed longer than she wanted to so we could continue to meet our obligations. The truth is these guys are a fussy bunch. They have someone specific in mind that they're looking for and Rex seems convinced that it's you."

"I'm flattered but I have no professional experience. I'm not sure what I can offer you. I didn't even know that I could sing until three years ago when some co-workers convinced me to come down to Bobbi-Jo's one evening with them. Normally I would have turned them down, but something made me go. I had so much fun and people seemed to like my singing, so I went back. Bobbi-Jo hired me to be a part of her House Band. I've been having fun there."

As Lily spoke, the men were all enraptured by her. Her voice had a bell-like quality to it. It was very melodic and clear. Her physical beauty did not escape anyone's attention. She was once again dressed in jeans and she wore an elegant blue sweater that brought out the blue in her eyes. A blue hairclip fastened her long blonde hair at the nape of her neck.

Lily continued to speak. "Someone gave me a tambourine to play while I wasn't singing, just to give me something to do to keep me on stage. I found it came naturally, so I have acquired several other percussion instruments and learned how and when to use them.

"Really though, I'm not sure about being a professional. I wouldn't know what to do. This is just a hobby."

Rex finally found his voice. "It's an amazing talent. It shouldn't be wasted on just a hobby."

"Maybe, but I have fun. Sometimes if a hobby turns into a job, it's no longer fun."

Benjamin cleared his throat to reassert his authority. "Would you be interested in at least hearing what we're looking for before you decide?"

Lily looked at everyone gathered around the table. They hung on her every word and she got the impression that they were willing to make many compromises to get her to sign with them.

"I find this a little uncomfortable and embarrassing," Lily said. "I need to understand why you are so desperate for an unknown that only one person in the room has actually heard and are so ready to believe in him."

"We're not desperate," repeated Benjamin.

"We're a family, Lily," Rex interrupted. "We've been together for a long time and we trust each other. We are willing to take each other's advice even if it seems strange sometimes. We give each other the benefit of the doubt. You would learn about that if this all worked out."

"What sort of things would be expected of me?"

Benjamin answered, "Threshold started out as a live act that recorded some CD's. Now they are a recording act that does live appearance to promote those CD's. We do several regular shows monthly around Illinois, Indiana and Wisconsin. We are planning a cross-country tour next year if sales continue to climb. If this goes well, we would like to go internationally. We would go to Canada and maybe Europe and Australia. We do charity events, we do studio recordings, we do television and radio appearances and there would be a lot of travel involved.

"Are you married?"

"No. I don't have any significant other."

"Do you have any children?"

"My only dependant is my cat."

"Do you have any other commitments that may cause a conflict with their schedule?"

"Like I mentioned to Rex the other night, I currently have two part-time jobs that pay my bills. I spend the rest of my time at home.

"I'm not sure I'm cut out for this sort of thing. I like my privacy. It sounds like the public are going to scrutinize Threshold under a microscope all the time. I would not be willing to do interviews or to divulge personal information about myself at any time to anyone. It would not be fair to throw me into a previously dug deep end and ask me to betray my very existence. You came to me. If I try out for this part, I will have to have some very strict guidelines set out to honor my conditions. I would need things in writing and I will maintain the ability to back out if it becomes more than I can personally handle. My lawyer will be involved from the beginning in every decision."

The five men looked at each other.

Rex asked, "Does this mean you're willing to consider trying out with us?"

Lily paused. "I'm willing to consider trying out. Nevertheless, I must insist on my private life remaining extremely private. I've seen what tabloids can do to people and I'm not interested in having my personal laundry, either fact or fiction, aired out publicly."

Benjamin sat down at the table. "I can't predict what the public will do. I will agree to your release if things are too much for you to handle. We will respect your privacy as much as we can control. Information obtained by the public will not come from this office or anyone in it. You will get that in writing. Tabloids and newspapers in general come up with their own works of fiction. Andy here is our resident expert on the tabloids. He buys them just to laugh at what is supposed to be happening in his life."

"It's a lot more interesting than my real life," Andy laughed.

"You will find a family here, if all goes well and you join us. The Threshold family is a very loyal and dependable bunch of people that far extends the people in this room. You may or may not want to be a part of it, but it's inevitable. We take care of our own and will give you as much privacy or support that you need. No one gets offended either way. We accept our differences and embrace each other regardless.

"Now, what do you say about performing with us sometime to see if we jive? I'll give you some CD's, if you don't already have them and a copy of the lyrics and music sheets."

"Never mind the music sheets. I couldn't read them anyway. Percussion is easy to fit it and I sing by ear. I will take the CD's and lyrics though."

Rex couldn't remain quiet any longer. "When can we be together?" He blushed. "I mean perform musically together."

"You guys can always come by Bobbi-Jo's on Wednesday...just for fun." Everyone laughed but agreed that it would be an excellent idea.

"One more question," Lily stated. "What kind of money are we talking about?"

Benjamin was anticipating that question. "We get various amounts for different types of performances. I take my cut off the top. The technical crew and security gets a fixed figure. What is left over is what the band takes home and that is split evenly among the band members."

"Evenly paid?" Lily was surprised. "You mean that if I joined, I would make as much as Mike or Rex or whoever has been around the longest and does the most amount of work."

"Mike and Rex get songwriters' royalties over and above what the gigs pay. As far as the rest of the band is concerned, this is how we have always done it and it will continue. If this works out, we'll work out a detailed contract outlining all of the small stuff.

"First, though, we've got to get you guys together. Jam at Bobbi-Jo's but I want a controlled tryout next week in our sound stage on the third floor. Can you come back next Friday afternoon to audition?"

"Meet here at three o'clock?" Lily asked. Benjamin nodded. "That sounds good. I have your card. If something comes up or I change my mind, I'll call."

"Anything else you want to know?"

"I'll let you know next week."

Everyone stood up as Lily rose from her seat. She gathered the CD's and files containing biographies of the band and the song lyrics. She once again smiled at everyone and moved toward the door. Benjamin was the first one there to open the door for her.

"Thanks again for coming in today," said Benjamin.

"Thank you all for inviting me in." She made eye contact with Rex and flashed him an extra smile. She waved as she left, leaving a trace of her perfume lingering in the room.

The men sat back down and there was complete silence for several minutes. Peter was the first one to speak.

"You said that Pam called you down to Bobbi-Jo's specifically to check out Lily?" he asked.

"Yeah," Rex responded. "Why?"

"Cindy would rather shoot me than introduce me to a woman like that!"

"Wow!" breathed Mike. "She definitely has sex appeal! I'm not sure we'd be able to work with her. She may just be a distraction!"

"Not to mention the wives killing us," added Benjamin.

"Oh, come on you guys!" Rex exclaimed. "Give her a chance! You didn't hear her or see her on stage. She is a natural. She's sexy. She has an incredible stage presence and unbelievable talent. I can hardly wait to play with her." He blushed again. "Musically that is."

Benjamin allowed himself to enjoy the moment. "It's been a long time since an unknown talent fell into my grasp. If I can make her into a star, she would be the icing on this old man's career.

"She doesn't want to be a star," said Rex. "She wants to have fun and this adventure may be too much for her to handle. Even though I'm convinced that she's the one we've been looking for, I guess we'll just have to wait and see what happens."

"I've got my fingers crossed," said Benjamin. "Good job, Rex."

Chapter Four

When Rex arrived home, Pam had already left for her meeting with the Bakers. He wanted to tell her how the meeting with Lily went. He was so excited that the rest of the group seemed to accept her and were willing to give her a chance. He never before felt so positive about the success of Threshold. He believed that within ten days, she would sign with them and the band would move forward with success they only dreamed. It seemed that he saw less and less of his wife and was finding it difficult to share his news with her.

Mike, meanwhile, was telling Cora over dinner all about the mysterious woman that Pam and Rex had discovered.

"She knows how to hold a room," declared Mike. "What's your schedule like Wednesday evening? I'd really appreciate your expert opinion about her."

"I'm working Wednesday," Cora replied, "but I'll see if I can get Jill to cover for me for a couple of hours. A lot is being put at stake on an unknown variable so it's important to me as well to get a reading on her." Cora grinned. "Besides, I want to check out the competition."

Wednesday evening at Bobbi-Jo's was the usual hustle of activity. Several people were already on stage even though it was only shortly after seven o'clock. Pam was sitting with the Bakers once again and they were quickly becoming very good friends. Mike arrived with Rex, who was carrying his guitar. They acknowledged Pam with a nod and a smile and she responded in kind. They sat at a nearby table and ordered drinks. Meanwhile, Benjamin arrived separately and as previously arranged, sat away from the guys from Threshold. They all anxiously waited for things to begin as they sipped their drinks.

Mike saw Bobbi-Jo and waved. She beamed a huge smile at him and rushed over to their table.

"Mikie!" she exclaimed. "I haven't seen you in ages! Are you too important now to visit little Bobbi-Jo? Is that it?"

Bobbi-Jo threw her arms around Mike and gave him a hug. She kissed both of his cheeks and then sat down next to him. She smiled at Rex and patted his hand.

"Now, B.J., you know that's not true," Mike reassured her. "I've just been really busy."

"Of course you are. Pam's not too busy to come and see Bobbi-Jo with her friends. Even here together, you are at separate tables. What's going on Mister?"

"Pam's got some new clients and she's enjoying their company and their business. I'm just as busy as Mike. I try to drop by once in awhile to check out potentially talented competition," Rex quipped.

"So, you bring your guitar tonight. Are you going to play with us?"

Mike answered, "Would you mind if we wanted to jam tonight? Do you think anyone would be offended?"

"Oh, my heavens, no!" exclaimed Bobbi-Jo. "Famous, handsome men such as yourselves want to play with the local little guys! It would be an honor and a thrill for everyone. We have some regulars who play every week and I'll bet you they would love to play with you. I'll catch you guys later. I'll go inform the ones that are here already!"

Bobbi-Jo left with a flamboyant wave and rushed over to the stage.

"You realize that everyone's going to make a big deal about us being here tonight."

"Let's just stick with the story. We're here to have some fun and relax."

Mike and Rex were still looking around for Lily when they saw Cora enter. Mike waved to get her attention and she smiled and approached.

"Hi, Babe!" Cora said as she leaned over and kissed Mike. "Hi, Rex."

"Hi."

"Was Jill able to cover for you?" Mike asked Cora.

"Yes, she's taking the rest of my shift. I'm returning the favor next week. I wouldn't miss this for anything. Where is this mystery woman?"

"She's not here yet."

"Maybe she got scared and won't show up."

"No, she's here now," said Rex and he nodded in Lily's direction.

Cora turned to see where Rex was indicating. There was no mistaking who she was looking for. Cora saw the tall blonde woman carrying her flowered case. Lily smiled at Bobbi-Jo, who was back by the bar. She made eye contact with Rex and Mike but didn't acknowledge that she knew them. She didn't want attention drawn to herself for being the reason they were there. By the time Lily had gotten to the stage, Bobbi-Jo was already there to greet her.

"You'd never guess who's here!"

"Who?"

"Threshold is here! At least, a couple of the guys are. I knew them all when they were kids and they came to hang out here tonight. This is going to be great for business. I know you'll have fun playing with them. They're very good you know. I have some more phone calls to make!"

Lily set up a percussion stand and her instruments. The other regular performers greeted her, tuned their instruments, and set up their things. As they settled, Bobbi-Jo came onto the stage and stood at the microphone.

"Good evening, everyone! Welcome to Bobbi-Jo's Jam Night. We have an exciting evening in store for you! First, I'll introduce our House Band. Johnny

Snow on keyboards. Lois Varner on bass. Barney Fitzpatrick on drums and The Flower Girl on percussion. Of course, they all sing too!

"It's going to be incredible tonight because we have some very special guests that will be jamming with us a little later. Some of the guys from local recording artist Threshold are here to party, so hold onto something because they will blow you away! Ladies and Gentlemen, Bobbi-Jo's House Band!"

As soon as Bobbi-Jo announced Threshold, cellular phones came out by the dozens. Rumors started circulating quickly that an impromptu concert was going to take place. The four regular performers started playing some songs from the Seventies and Eighties. Other performers started to come up onto the stage and replaced the regulars. They performed various styles and songs. Some of the performers were quite good and others were not. It was fun to watch and memories were abounding for Mike, Rex and Pam.

Within the hour, the club was packed. Crowds gathered around the bar, around the stage and on the dance floors. People spotted Mike and Rex and were pointing and gossiping. Meanwhile, Mike, Rex, Cora and Benjamin were intently watching Lily's style on stage. They heard the power and range of her vocals. They saw her interaction with the crowd and others on stage. They watched as she took center stage and all the attention as she belted out solos. They watched as she flirted with the other performers as she danced around them with her percussions and sang duos. They were also impressed how she lost herself into the background when she wasn't the center of attention and didn't upstage those who were displaying their stuff. She enhanced every song that she participated in with her vocals and her percussive abilities.

After another hour, Rex and Mike decided it was time to join the action. Rex removed his guitar from its carrying case and they stood. Bobbi-Jo had been watching for them to move and when she saw them, she ran over to the stage and picked up a spare microphone.

"Is everyone having fun?" bellowed Bobbi-Jo.

The crowd cheered loudly.

"Are you ready for our special guests?"

The crowd cheered, whistled, and banged bottles and glasses.

"Ladies and Gentlemen, Mike Mitchell and Rex Landers from Threshold!"

The crowd went wild. The club was packed and there was a lot of excitement. Mike caught Cora's attention and winked at her. Rex found Pam and smiled at her. They both saw Benjamin back at the bar. He had moved from his table, presumably to get a better view of the stage. Lily smiled at them both. Mike took the microphone from Bobbi-Jo and put his arm around her.

"Hello, everyone!" Mike shouted. The crowd cheered again.

"You may be wondering why we're here tonight. Well, we wanted to pay tribute to Bobbi-Jo who let us adorn her stage many times when we were young pups and she gave us chances that no one else would for a long time. Bobbi-Jo, we wanted to thank you for all you've done for Threshold and for many young talented people out there who can come here to showcase their stuff; past, present and future."

The crowd cheered again.

"Also, you may know that we released a new CD a few months ago and you may have heard our singles on the radio and seen our video on TV. We want to announce that within the next several months, we are planning a cross country tour and next year we hope to go International."

Again, the crowd went wild.

"Now, these are just some things we're thinking about, but it's you, the fans that can make it possible. Keep supporting all the local talent here at Bobbi-Jo's! Special thanks go to all of you! People like you make a band like Threshold as successful as we are. Thank you!"

As the crowd continued to make a lot of noise, Mike and Rex started to play one of their popular songs. The performers quickly picked up "Dancing Angel" and played it well. Many songs followed, some by Threshold, but mainly other popular songs current and past. Rex wowed them with his skills on his guitar and Mike sang. Johnny offered him his keyboard, but he refused. He was having fun just singing without the responsibility of playing as well. He wanted to interact with Lily without a keyboard in the way. The connection between them was instantaneous and strong. It was almost as if they had been performing together for years. The audience felt the connection and encouraged it with their cheers. Everyone had a few too many drinks but the mood was jovial and celebratory.

From her table, Cora looked on at the chemistry between her husband and this beautiful woman. She couldn't deny how real it was. She knew their twelve-year marriage was strong; however, she couldn't help feel a bit disconcerted. Mike and Lily were dancing and singing together as if it was the most natural thing in the world. Rex also played and interacted with Lily well. With time, the three of them would make an extremely alluring team on stage.

Cora decided to find out Pam's opinion so she went over to the Bakers' table. Pam wasn't there so she asked George of her whereabouts. George told her that she left for home. Cora came to the immediate realization that Lily was going to be a very real part of all their lives from this point forward. She knew that these musical collaborations and personal relationships were just beginning and would be around for years to come.

Chapter Five

The members of Threshold had met at Beady Eye offices an hour before Lily was due to arrive. They wanted to discuss amongst themselves the occurrences of Wednesday evening at Bobbi-Jo's and to discuss ideas for a contract to offer her. Benjamin once again had taken command of the meeting.

"The first thing I have to say is that I am in full agreement with Rex. Lily's the missing link that Threshold has been looking for from the beginning, even if we didn't realize we were looking for it. She is definitely the one. Her talent, her energy, her personality and even her appearance all fit in perfectly with Threshold's image and sound. Theresa is awesome, but let's face it, since we have to replace her, we should get a completely different talent that will blow everyone away.

"It's already been agreed upon that she'll earn the same as Theresa, which is one-fifth of what the band takes home. Mike, are you ready to be upstaged by this beauty?"

"From what I could tell on Wednesday," Mike answered, "she didn't upstage anyone when she wasn't supposed to. When she was singing lead, she commanded everyone's attention however when she had to share the spotlight, she did that without upstaging her partner. When she was singing back up or just playing percussion, she was almost non-existent. I didn't think that type of person even existed, let alone a stage performer."

Benjamin continued, "I agree. It was definitely refreshing not to have an ego-centric personality to deal with. Road accommodations would have to be the same as Theresa. The lone female performer must have special privileges while you low-life men will have to share rooms."

"I can think of a few guys traveling with us that wouldn't mind sharing a room with Lily," Andy said.

Benjamin and Peter laughed, but Rex took offence.

"If Lily joins us, it will be a complete change for her," Rex explained. "She'd be giving up her entire way of life because we asked her to. Remember, we sought her out. She didn't come to us looking for any favors. I should hope that everyone will give her the respect and consideration any other one of us had with each other. We need to accept her and treat her as one of the Threshold family. I hope we'll all be mature enough to work with her as an equal without distractions."

"It looks like she's got a big brother already," Peter said.

"She will have a lot of brothers," Benjamin apologized. "Rex is correct. She didn't come to us. We're practically begging her to join us. We will be very lenient and generous. This is foreign territory for her. She has no idea what she's getting herself into so we'll have to make this transition as easy as possible for her. We're old pros and we have to remember that."

"Speak for yourselves," added Peter. "Some of us aren't old."

They continued to discuss various ideas and options for Lily until the intercom buzzed. Ruth announced Lily's arrival. "Show her in," Benjamin ordered.

The door opened and Ruth came in with Lily. Lily looked uncomfortable.

"Ruth," Benjamin said, "please take Lily's bag. Try to find Tony and get him to take it down to the sound stage. Thanks."

Ruth took Lily's case and left, closing the door behind her once again.

"Thank you so much for coming back," Benjamin beamed. "Please sit down for a moment."

Once again, Peter stood and pulled a chair out for her.

"Thanks, Peter," Lily said.

Peter blushed as he sat. Andy disguised a chuckle by coughing and Benjamin frowned at him.

"We were very impressed with your performance Wednesday evening. Rex wasn't exaggerating a bit when he told us about you. It was a thrill to watch you on stage and Mike and Rex confirm that it was just as must fun to perform with you."

"Thanks. I also had a lot of fun. Mike, it's amazing to sing with you. It was effortless. I was surprised."

"Actually," Mike added, "it was very comfortable. I felt like we could have done anything and you would have kept up with whatever we threw at you."

"We made a good team," Lily agreed.

Benjamin interrupted, "We invited you back today to hit the sound stage. I almost feel that it's unnecessary, but we're all here and I have a crew compliment of five guys anxious to get some rehearsal in. In addition, Andy and Peter haven't had the privilege of being on stage with you, so maybe we should officially do that audition. Are you up for that right now?"

"That's what I came here for. I must admit that I'm extremely nervous. This is so new to me. I'm excited, but nervous. I've always had an audience to feed off of and it certainly never mattered if I messed up."

"It still doesn't matter. These guys mess up all the time," joked Benjamin. "Every show has a few screw-ups."

"It's usually me," offered Peter. "When I auditioned, I did all right and the guys here reassured me that I fit in well with their style and personality. After they hired me, they practically had to carry me through the first few shows. I was so nervous; I couldn't keep a beat or find my strings. They didn't kick me out though. They kept their faith in me and I'm still here…and I still make mistakes."

Lily laughed. "Thanks Peter. That's comforting."

Benjamin stood up. Everyone else followed his lead. "Let's go up then to level three, shall we?"

Once inside the sound stage studio, Lily felt even more uncomfortable. It was very quiet and there were a few people fussing over lights and sound gear. Her case had been brought down, as requested by Benjamin and sat on the stage unopened. Benjamin escorted her to the stage and a technician approached them.

"Excuse me, Ma'am. My name's Tony Sebastien and I'm in charge of these techno-monkeys around here. I didn't open your case because I didn't have your permission. I understand you have percussion instruments to set up."

"Yes, I do. I don't have many, just the few that I like to use on a regular basis. It's everything I own though," Lily confessed.

"No worries," Tony reassured her. "Come with me and we'll get you set up."

Benjamin followed Tony and Lily as she picked up her case and went to the spot that Tony pointed out to her.

"Mike always has up front and center with his microphone and keyboards. Andy sets up on the platform at the back, again in the center. Peter is stage right and Rex is stage left. Andy is the only one who doesn't have a microphone. We try to discourage him from singing," Tony joked.

"I heard that!" Andy yelled.

"You were supposed to!" Tony laughed.

Benjamin took Lily by the arm and guided her away a short distance. He looked at Tony and Andy and, while smiling, pretended to be angry. "Now, children, leave it at home. We have a guest." He winked at Lily and she returned his smile.

Tony approached and took Lily by her other arm. "Unhand her, Mr. Dapril. I'm not finished with the lady yet."

Benjamin acted injured and let go. "Just give her back when you're done."

"Benji's a little possessive of his new stars," Tony said. "As I was saying, Theresa used to wander around with a cordless mike. She didn't play anything, so she had the freedom to go wherever she pleased. You, however play percussion, so we'd like to set you up between Mike and Rex. You'll be the Lily Rose between two thorns," Tony laughed. "We can get you a headset style mike if you want to roam and continue to play, but you'd also have a station for your gear and a fixed mike at which to stand. How does that sit with you?"

"Like I said, this is all new to me. Whatever works for you guys, just tell me and I'll accommodate you."

"Do you have a certain set up for your instruments?"

"I can just leave them in my case and dig out whatever I need, whenever I need it. At Bobby-Jo's, I just borrow one of their stands."

"I'd like to get something for you, once I see you in action. After I get an idea of what you use and how you move around, I'll get a stand that you can place each item on so it's at your ready disposal. What do you use the most?"

"My tambourine gets used a lot. I also like my cowbell and woodblock. Of course, I also interchange anything with maracas or a cabaça. I'm also a leftie, it that helps at all."

"That's what I need to know! Once everyone has set up, we'll go through a typical show. This is also a rehearsal for the lighting and sound technicians as well. We have a couple of newbie's with us so you're not alone here. We perform each song a couple of times and we can get comfortable with where everyone fits in. Over the next few weeks, you'll get familiar with song lists, solos, breaks and general organization of the whole show. For now, this is just a basic rehearsal and audition so just take things as they come and relax. Have fun. Nothing's at stake today."

"Thanks, Tony. You've been a big help."

"I'm the one you come to with any and all problems, questions and complaints." Tony smiled. "I've heard great things about you Miss Rose. It's an honour to be able to work with you."

Benjamin had relocated to behind the soundboard. Tony waved at him.

"We're all ready here, Mr. Dapril! Whenever the band is set, we'll get the sound check done."

Benjamin gave him a thumbs-up sign. Tony turned back to Lily.

"Are you ready?"

"I'm as ready as I'll ever be. I could use a drink though."

Tony smiled and patted her arm gently. "You'll be fine. If this goes well, I'm sure Benji will take you out personally for dinner and a bottle of Champaign."

He looked at the others on the stage as they put final tunings and set-ups on their gear. With a final smile at Lily, Tony jumped off the stage and began to shout instructions to his team. She organized her things so that she would be comfortable. Another technician jumped up onto the stage, set a sheet of paper at each microphone, and secured it with gaffer's tape. She saw that it was a song list. He then clipped a small microphone onto the mike stand lower than her vocal mike to that it would pick up the percussion sounds.

Lily had a whole flock of butterflies in her stomach. She wished that she had had a little more to drink before she came but she didn't want to arrive drunk and ruin her chance at this opportunity. She closed her eyes and took several deep breaths, trying to put out of her mind that everyone in that room was there because of her.

Lily got scared. She considered apologizing for wasting their time and leaving. She started to panic. She felt suddenly that she had gotten herself into something that she wasn't capable of accomplishing. She wasn't a performer. These people were being very kind to her. They had faith that she could provide a missing ingredient in something that wasn't missing in the first place. They thought that she could replace a member who was integral in making this band a success. She knew that her demons would resurface and ruin her and she didn't want to take this band down with her. She could not hide the truth from them for long.

"Are you ready?" asked Mike.

Lily startled. She nodded and smiled. She heard Tony's voice through the stage monitors.

"We're going to do sound checks now. We'll start with you Mike."

Each performer did a sound check with their instruments and vocal mike so Tony could get proper levels and sound quality for each on the soundboard. Lily did her sound check in turn and decided that since she was already there, she would do her best and take things as they came, one step at a time.

Chapter Six

Back downstairs in the conference room, Benjamin, Mike, Rex, Andy, Peter and Lily sat once again around the table. They were discussing their performance of Threshold's material. All agreed that Lily fit in extremely well with them. Lily herself confessed that she was surprisingly very comfortable despite making many mistakes during the songs.

"You've never done these songs before," Benjamin said to Lily. "It was to be expected that there would be a few glitches. During rehearsals we'll go through each song, line by line if necessary until everyone is comfortable with what their doing.

"We've got some upcoming shows next month. That leaves only a few weeks to work out everything. You'll be fine by then. What's your week like next week?"

"I still have my part-time jobs in the evenings, but during the days I'm fairly free, I guess," Lily answered.

"You'll have to give up the evening jobs, I'm afraid. Can you start on Monday? Are you available around one o'clock?"

"Wait. Are you telling me that you're accepting me?"

"We sure are! Congratulations. You are the newest member of the Threshold family!"

Lily sighed with relief and concern. "I'm a little nervous and confused. This is all happening so fast. I enjoy this. I'm just concerned about what this is going to do to my life."

Rex leaned forward and patted her hand. "Just relax and go with the flow. We'll go over all of your concerns and see what we can do to make you more comfortable and confident that you're not making the biggest mistake of your life."

"I've always been a very private person," repeated Lily. "I'm actually quite shy and don't open up to people easily. Let's just say I have a major trust issue. It's difficult for me to tell you that much. I don't mind being on stage performing because there's an imaginary boundary there. I don't have to let anyone in. I can maintain my anonymity. I leave and don't answer to anyone.

"I'm concerned about the publicity that this band gets. I'm not too fond of the thought of attention from strangers. I understand that this will be part of the experience. I'm just not sure I'll know how to handle it."

"Unfortunately or fortunately, depending on how you look at it," Benjamin interjected, "this band is very popular as you said. We can shelter you quite a bit. You don't have to commit to any radio or television interviews. Mike and Rex usually handle those.

"We can't promise you how your fans are going to react. I think they are going to love you and they are going to want to know just whom Lily Rose is. We'll write up a biography together that you'd be happy to release and Andy can update the website. You're replacing someone that Threshold fans have grown accustomed to and love. This office will release a statement within the next couple of weeks to disclose where Theresa went and who you are. There's also the matter of a new band photo for the posters and website."

"I want you all to understand," Lily continued, "that I'm coming on board with a lot of baggage. There are a lot of problems and issues in my life that I'm not going to be willing to discuss or disclose for that matter. If you want me, you have to take me, as I am, problems and all. I don't want any lectures a few weeks from now on changes I need to make."

"I'm sure we can handle anything that comes up," Rex stated. "If it doesn't affect your performance or the band or our safety, we'll deal with it. Who knows? Maybe as you get used to being a part of a new family, we may be able to support you or help you in some way."

"Again," Lily insisted, "I do not open up to people easily."

"That's all right," Rex reassured her. "Just give us the same chance we're giving you. I believe this is going to be a great experience for all of us."

"I don't want my surname to be used at all, either," Lily added.

"Rose?" asked Benjamin.

"No. My last name is Delphinium."

"I have you in my records as 'Lily Rose'. I didn't even realize that you had another name. Lily Rose Delphinium. What a beautiful name. Someone sure liked flowers when they named you. Don't worry. We'll keep you as Lily Rose if that's what you want. We should discuss payment, touring schedules and all the other stuff that needs to be talked about."

They spent another two hours going over details then everyone went home for the weekend. On Monday, everyone met to practice at one o'clock. Lily quickly became even more comfortable with the rest of the band and worked hard on learning the songs. By Wednesday, she was familiar with all the material and had the percussion flawless. Lyrics were still a problem, but she was on her way to mastering those as well.

On Thursday, they met again at the scheduled time. However, Andy was late. They sat and chatted about a variety of subjects. Lily sat apart from the others, quietly sipping a bottle of cola. Mike saw this so he approached her. As he did, she quickly put the cap on the bottle and smiled.

"Where are you parking?" asked Mike.

"I don't have a car."

"You don't?" Mike asked in surprise. "How have you been getting here with all your stuff?"

"I usually take a taxi."

"That just won't do! You carry a lot of expensive gear. We can't have you roaming around with it in taxis. It's not safe, especially when we start doing shows all over the place and late at night. We'll get you a car."

"I can't get a car," said Lily. "I can't drive."

"We'll get you lessons and you can learn."

"You don't understand," Lily stood up quickly and lost her balance. She grabbed the chair and held onto it. "I can't drive! I don't want to have to explain! Just accept the fact that I can't drive!"

Lily turned to walk away, but walked into a microphone stand, knocking it over. Mike quickly caught it, stunned at her agitation.

"All right," Mike conceded. "Relax. No questions, just as we promised. We'll have someone take you home and pick you up."

"I don't want to be a nuisance. I can manage travel arrangements."

"It's more of a nuisance for you to try to arrange transportation than it would be for one of us to drive you to and from shows and rehearsals. Where do you live?"

Lily gave Mike her address.

"Rex and Tony both live in that direction. One of them probably wouldn't mind driving you around. Any one of us will do it."

Lily started to object, but Mike stopped her. "No further discussion. Consider it arranged."

"Thanks," Lily said shyly. "I would appreciate it."

Andy then arrived carrying a tabloid magazine. He waved it at everyone.

"We've made the latest edition of 'Weekly Gab'. There's an article about us on page six, photo included. I'm sorry about this, Lily. It didn't take long for you to get attention."

Lily sat back down hard in the chair and dropped her cola bottle. She picked it up and fiddled with it. Andy showed the page to them.

"I'll read some of it for you.

"'Threshold Woos New Singer.

"'Last week, several members of the Chicago-based popular recording artists Threshold arrived at a local nightclub for an impromptu performance. The local musicians and audience were in for a special treat when keyboard player and singer Mike Mitchell arrived to jam on stage. Threshold guitar player Rex Landers also was on stage for most of the evening.

"'The two leaders of Threshold linked up with a local favorite known as The Flower Girl. Patrons confirmed that this woman, whose name may be Lily, has been a regular performer for three years. Rumors say that Threshold manager Benjamin Dapril was also on hand to check out the talented beauty. Apparently, the men from Threshold were so impressed with The Flower Girl that they offered her a position with the band, ousting long-time band member Theresa MacKenzie.'

"It goes on to say that Theresa is suing all of us as well as Bobbi-Jo for allowing all this to happen. Theresa is supposedly threatening Lily as well."

"I'm sorry Lily," Rex said. "You're getting a taste of this nastiness before you're even officially announced as a part of Threshold. I can't believe people write this stuff."

Mike laughed. "I can't believe people buy this stuff," he said while elbowing Andy in the ribs.

"I can't believe trees die for this stuff," Lily said.

"Are you alright with this?" Rex asked Lily.

"I won't lie. It bothers me. It's weird though how facts can be distorted and people believe the ounce of truth that's in it as gospel."

"As long as the people who are important in your life know the truth, the rest is just garbage and mostly everyone knows it. We just ignore it and feel sorry for those who need to believe this stuff. Mostly it's harmless."

"I worry about the ones who aren't harmless," Lily muttered quietly.

Benjamin stepped into the conversation. "You will always be well guarded at all of the shows. If there is an issue with fans, Threshold's security will be there. All venues also have their own added security teams. If it's away from venues, keep a cell phone handy and call the police. They are generally good with their response time. It shouldn't come to that though.

"We want you with us. I think you'll have a lot of fun with us. Theresa and some of the wives had stuff printed about them, but nothing serious ever came of it. They just brushed it off and it went away."

Cautiously reassured, Lily joined them on stage to rehearse. Soon, she forgot the tabloid and sang her best. She was feeling very good and knew almost all of the lyrics and combined them with her percussion. She and Mike enjoyed playing off each other. They bantered, danced and even flirted with each other. During duets, they sang to each other enthusiastically. During love ballads, people would have thought that they were in love with each other as they leaned against each other and stared dreamily into each other's eyes.

Unknown to Lily and Mike, Cora had arrived quietly and sat at the back of the room. She observed the interaction between her husband and the sexy new singer. Being as observant as she was, she knew that it was all an act. Fans and tabloids would eat it up. She knew Mike better than anyone else and never worried about his behavior with other women. His passionate act with Lily would be great for the success of Threshold. She also observed that Lily's eyes were glazed and unfocused and she was unstable on her feet. She looked as if she would topple over.

The band took a break from rehearsing. Everyone scattered to do his or her own thing. Lily took her purse and her ever-present bottle of cola and went to the bathroom. While in the privacy of the stall, she took out a bottle of pills and swallowed some. When she was through in the bathroom, she washed up, touched up her lipstick, chewed a fresh piece of gum and rejoined the others.

Cora was chatting with Mike and Rex. Lily went over to say hello. She staggered a bit and put her arms around both men.

"That was a great performance!" said Cora.

Lily blushed. "You don't mind the way I carry on with Mike?"

"It's different. Theresa didn't do any of that. It adds a lot more excitement and energy. You're fitting in well. How do you feel?"

"I'm having a wonderful time. I never had so much fun at a job. I can't believe I can even call it a job."

Lily walked away and Mike leaned over and whispered to Cora.

"Well, what do you think?"

"I'm a bit concerned."

"You know this is harmless flirting."

"It's not that. You do realize that she's stoned out of her mind."

"She's a bit drunk."

"She's stoned and you know it," Cora repeated. "No one can deny it. Everyone can smell the booze on her breath but she's been taking some sort of drug as well. She is as high as a kite. She'll work out well with the band if she keeps her substance abuse under control. Sorry, but you asked for my opinion. You don't want Threshold to get a reputation for encouraging drug use. "

After the rehearsal was over, Tony checked the equipment and began to wrap mike cables. Lily hesitated nearby. Sensing that she wanted to speak to him, Tony stopped and smiled at her. She returned his smile and walked over to him.

Tony asked, "How are you getting along?"

"Things are going a lot better than I had expected them to," Lily replied. "These guys are easy to play with. I feel right at home here."

"The Threshold family makes everyone feel that way. We all become a part of it. It's hard to explain, but no one seems to be able to escape from it," Tony laughed. "We all take care of each other, whether we want help or not."

"I know we only met last week, but you told me that if I ever needed anything, I could come to you and ask for help."

"I certainly did and I meant it. Just name it and it's yours."

Lily hesitated. "Did you mean musically speaking or anything at all?"

Tony had noticed her condition and discomfort. He knew she was asking for something that might not be easy to ask for.

"I get the impression that that asking for help with something doesn't come naturally for you."

"I'm a very private person and there are many aspects of my life that are extremely personal. I have trouble trusting people."

"No worries here," Tony reassured her. "I'm a very discreet person myself. You can trust me. I can get you anything your little heart desires. Just ask."

Lily felt uncomfortable, but she smiled.

Chapter Seven

Winter broke in the middle of November with a blizzard that immobilized Chicago. Threshold cancelled their rehearsals. Lily decided to practice in her music room with the CD's that Benjamin had given her. She was very confident that she could handle the upcoming shows. If only her head didn't ache so much, she would feel even more confident.

As she took a break and went to the kitchen to get another drink, Lily was surprised to hear a knock at her front door. She opened the door to find a snow covered Tony.

"What are you doing out in this storm? Come in!"

Tony entered her foyer and stamped the snow off his boots.

"Give me your jacket and gloves. I'll hang them in the laundry room. I have some coffee made in the kitchen. Help yourself. Mugs are in the cupboard over the coffee-maker."

Tony took off his boots and went into the kitchen. He found the mugs and poured himself a cup of hot coffee. He felt himself begin to warm up from the inside as he drank. He looked around Lily's kitchen. It was very clean and impressive. Her house had two levels and an attached single car garage. A hallway extended from the kitchen to the back of the house, obviously to the laundry room and garage.

Lily returned to the kitchen. She picked up her mug and motioned with it to the table.

"Please, have a seat."

Tony sat at her solid oak round table that had a white tile top. The four chairs were made of matching oak. He also noticed that the cupboards were also made of oak. As he drank his coffee, he was admiring the quality of workmanship in the room when something touched his leg and he jumped.

"Oh! What was that?" Tony exclaimed, startled.

Lily began to laugh. "Silly human," she said as she bent down and retrieved a black and white cat from under the table. "Did Jackson scare the silly human?" she crooned to the cat as she rubbed his ears. The cat meowed loudly and began to purr.

"We don't get many guests here so Jackson takes advantage of as much attention as he can get. I guess he's my alter-ego."

Tony made some idle talk about the house and the stainless steel appliances. He questioned her on the ceramic tiles in the kitchen and the hardwood floors throughout the lower level. Lily felt uncomfortable with Tony in her home, so she decided to stop the small talk.

"What brings you here? It's a miserable day."

"I'm on my way to Springfield to meet with some people. If you want those pain killers, it'll cost six-hundred dollars for one hundred."

"That's six dollars a pill!"

"If you're in a hurry for them, that's what they'll cost. I got the impression that you needed them sooner as opposed to later, or you wouldn't have asked someone you knew only for a few days to get them for you. I can keep looking around but you can have these by tomorrow."

Lily was silent. She needed something for the pain and she didn't want to be sick during rehearsals or the shows.

Tony continued, "If you don't mind me asking, how long this supply will last you? If I know in advance, it won't be such short notice and you might not pay as much."

"It depends on how much my head hurts. Some days are worse than others are. I don't know how many I take." Lily paused. "So, how does this work? Do I give you the money now or later?"

"I don't have that kind of money. Nothing personal, but I don't shell out any money for someone else and risk being stuck with product I don't use. I'd need the money now."

"I really don't like doing this," Lily confessed, "however my doctor won't write me any more prescriptions."

"Have you tried multiple doctors?"

"I tried that but the pharmacies are all linked now by computer. Red flags went off and now I'm cut off."

"It doesn't seem medically responsible to cut a patient off of meds that she clearly needs."

"Well, I'm not cut off completely. It's just that I take a few more than I should and my doctor thinks I should cut back. The problem is the pain doesn't cut back."

"Have no fear, my dear," Tony said, "This time tomorrow you'll have a new supply. I need to leave soon though if I'm going to make it in time for my appointment with the roads the way they are. Do you have the money on hand?"

"I have some tucked away. Wait here."

Lily went up the staircase that was in the foyer. Tony took the opportunity to look through her house a little more. The dining room had a large oak table with six elegant high backed chairs, covered with a light sage material on the seats. An oak buffet and hutch adorned the end of the room and contained silver candlesticks and a silver tea set. A crystal chandelier hung over the table and an exquisite oriental rug with hues of green and brown lay beneath. It seemed that all rooms had oak blinds with sage green sheers and matching valances.

The living room was just as tidy and elegant. A dark brown leather sofa and matching chair and ottoman furnished it. A rectangular oak cocktail table sat in front of the sofa on a light brown area rug while matching end tables stood on either side of the sofa. Two large framed oil paintings hung on the wall behind the sofa. They were a two-part painting of deer in a meadow with a lake reflecting the mountains and sunset. A hexagon shaped oak curio cabinet sat in a corner displaying a collection of fine lead crystal.

Tony heard Lily coming back down the stairs so he met her at the bottom of the stairs.

"I was just admiring your home," he told Lily. "It's so clean and tidy and it's beautifully decorated."

"Thanks."

Lily handed Tom an envelope.

"There's six hundred dollars in there. I'm not very comfortable doing this," Lily repeated.

"Don't worry. You have a need and I can supply you with a solution. I'll drop by tomorrow with your purchase. Will you be all right until then?"

"Yes, I've got some. You didn't tell your 'friends' who these were for, did you?"

"No. Your name will never cross my lips when I'm dealing with my 'friends'? I promise you that."

"Thanks again. You'll drive safely in this storm?"

"I will. I had better get going. Can you get my things?"

Lily retrieved his wet clothing and watched as he left. She bolted the door and felt nauseous. She was definitely hitting a new low in her desperation. She knew she needed to get a grip on her drug use, but the pain was unbearable most days. She decided that she could handle it and went to the living room to pour herself yet another drink.

Chapter Eight

The Threshold concerts were selling out as quickly as the tickets were going on sale. Interviews and photographs were constantly in demand. As per her contract, Lily did not do any interviews although the public wanted to know who the new girl was. If anything, her mysteriousness added to her charm and appeal. There was little she could do about the photographers snapping pictures of her when she was out. It was unnerving, but so far, it was harmless.

The band members would meet at Beady Eye Productions and Andy would drive them all in the company van to the local venues or cities in which they were playing. Tony volunteered to pick up Lily at her house to take her to Beady Eye and drove her home afterward. A truck with all the instruments, sound gear and lighting equipment left for the show in advance of the band. Tony entrusted his team to do the set up and tear down. He checked everything carefully when he arrived and ran the show. He often joked about being the boss and doing the least amount of work. In truth, he worked harder mentally while he was there and running the show than the men and women doing the physical work.

The first two shows were very hectic. Even though Lily was the newest member, they all made mistakes. Miscues were commonplace but the crowds never seemed to notice or care. Threshold was gaining popularity with every show. The interaction between Mike and Lily drove the crowd wild. Naturally, the tabloids covered every move with intimate details of the 'affair' between them. Lily often expressed concern, but neither Mike nor Cora minded. They were having fun and were never closer in their marriage.

The band continued to have regular rehearsals between the shows and tried to fine-tune their material. It tended to be stressful and everyone was quick tempered. No one blamed anyone else for the mistakes, but they were all irritable with each other.

Demands for their performances decreased over the Christmas holidays. They took some time off to celebrate the holidays and most went away or stayed quietly at home with their families. Lily had nowhere to go and no one to spend it with, so she spent a quiet few days at home. The pain wasn't as bad, but she found herself drinking a lot to pass the time and dull the loneliness. As quickly as the holidays arrived, they seemed to end and Threshold was once again traveling all over several states playing at least two and sometimes three shows per week.

Lily found that the psychological stress and the physical demands of the singing, dancing and traveling aggravated her headaches. The painkillers that Tony had obtained for her through that unknown and most likely disreputable source were becoming less and less effective. The more immune her body became to the pills, the more she required to dull the pain. She asked Tony to get her more. Her drinking and marijuana use increased as well and before long, everyone who worked with Threshold was aware that she was seriously out of control with her substance abuse. They were all very concerned for her personal well-being.

By early March, Benjamin decided to call a meeting of the band without Lily involved. He also included Tony who not only played a key role on the team, but who also was the one to spend the most time with her away from the stage.

"Gentlemen," began Benjamin, "first of all, I want to express my displeasure of having to hold a band meeting while intentionally excluding a very key member. Thank you all for coming and not letting Lily know about this. We all know what's going on with her and we're all concerned. She may have only been with us a few months and I can only speak for myself, but I think we all have become quite enamored with Lily and she's now a big part of our family.

"Lily has probably had this problem for quite some time. I'm not an expert, I thankfully have never battled the demons that she is, and we have no idea how long she has had this problem. She said she was coming on board with baggage and this is probably it. She specified a non-interference clause in her contract with us so we are limited officially to what we can do with her. We can't make her stop nor can we force her into rehab.

"At the same time, we need to consider Threshold's image. What's more, we need to intervene or she's going to kill herself. At the very least, she's going to be so sick and incapacitated that she won't be any good to anyone, including herself. I don't know about you guys, but I don't want to go through this again. I can't stand to lose another young, beautiful and talented woman."

A lot of emotion was in the room. Rex wiped a tear and no one said anything. He was remembering someone dear and special he had lost a few years previously.

"Lily needs intervention," Benjamin continued, "and if not us then who? Tony, you seem to be the closest to Lily. She has taken to you quite a bit and you spend a great deal of time with while her driving her back and forth. Is there anything you can tell us that might help?"

Tony looked at his hands. He assumed they called him into this meeting to discuss his own problem with substance abuse. He didn't want to draw attention to himself, but he too cared about Lily. If it meant disclosing his most personal secrets to get her help, he had to do it. It was not an easy decision to make. He was quiet for a long time, but his friends knew that he was battling with something. They were not going to force him to do or disclose anything.

"Actually, guys," Tony started, "I'm not the one to ask for help here. If anything, I may be a big part of the problem. I don't want to reveal personal stuff. Lily would be furious with me."

"I'd rather her furious than dead," exclaimed Rex. "Please tell us anything that can help."

Tony stared at his hands. "We may spend a lot of time together, but it's not exactly quality time."

Rex began to get impatient. "If you and Lily have a thing going, that's fine. It's none of our business. If it's not going smoothly, that's between you guys as well. You seem to be the only one that she has let into her life. We need to reach her and if that's through you, then we have to use you. I'm sorry to interfere, but we need to do something."

Tony looked up. "I get the impression that she's been hurt really badly and I don't think she's really going to let anyone in her life any time soon, especially a man. We're not having a relationship. We get together to drink and get high. She considers me someone safe. She knows I won't try to hurt her." He paused. "It's kind of ironic that she thinks I'm safe to be with, but the truth is, I'm the one enabling and supplying her."

A shocked silence filled the conference room. No one knew what to say. Rex was the first to find his voice.

"What exactly have you been supplying her with?" Rex asked.

"Pain killers and marijuana mainly and some booze. I justified supplying her with those things because I thought if she didn't get them from me, she might turn to someone else who didn't care about her and get into something worse like heroin or cocaine or something."

"How long have you been supplying her?" Rex asked.

"A week after she joined us, she came to me to find out if I could get her some painkillers. She suffers from bad headaches and I think she guessed that I might be someone who could help her. How she guessed, I don't know."

"How did you get her to trust you?" asked Benjamin.

"I don't know if she really trusts me at all. She just knows who I am. I think she's fine as long as she knows who she's dealing with and what she can expect and how far she can let herself go."

"If she seems to be scared of men, how did you convince her to let you in," Benjamin continued.

"She knows that I'm not interested in her."

"But you're young and single."

Tony paused once again.

"She knows that I'm gay."

Once again, there was a shocked silence.

"Why did you not tell us sooner?" asked Peter.

"It wasn't anyone's business. It still isn't. I've been traveling with you guys for the last few years and often I share a room with some of you. If you knew that I was gay, would you have been comfortable doing that?"

Again, silence reigned.

"I didn't think so," Tony said. "I've been using for years and I thought Lily was just a fun person to get high with. I didn't see her as being in a crisis state.

I never thought about it until a few weeks ago. I then started to realize that this was more than just having a good time."

"What happened a few weeks ago?" asked Mike.

"I didn't get her pain killers. I figured she would wait a few more days until I could get to my supplier to get them. She freaked on me. She demanded that I take her directly to my supplier immediately and that she didn't trust me with her money anymore. I worried about the harder stuff she could fall into so I complied.

"We got into my car and drove down to Springfield. Meanwhile she started asking for anything that would give her a buzz. I don't normally carry stuff in my car unless I've done a purchase. I didn't have anything with me that night. She nagged at me for a while and panicked but then she got quiet. I thought she had just given up venting, but when I looked over at her, she was very pale. Her eyes were twitching and she was sweating. She was going into a withdrawal shock right there in my car.

"I found a place where we could get a few drinks. She seemed to recover a bit, but she was far from well. I asked her if I should take her to a hospital but she refused. She said that she was fine. We got to Springfield, she paid for her pills not even caring that she was revealing her identity to unsavory characters and I took her home. When I picked her up for rehearsal a few days later, it was as if nothing out of the ordinary even happened.

"I am not ashamed to admit that I was really scared. I didn't know what to do. Now here you guys are asking me to help her. Maybe just being able to finally get what happened off of my chest is the only way I can help her."

Everyone sat quietly stunned.

Benjamin stood up and ran his hands through his hair. "Wow. I knew it was bad, but I had no idea that it was this bad." He turned to the rest of the men. "We may be over our heads here."

Mike spoke up. "We already know a lot about this stuff. The first thing is that she will have to want to get help. To do that, she would have to admit to having a problem. Problems like these usually start out with a specific event or events. If we could get close enough to her to find out what has happened to her in her mysterious past, maybe then we can work on getting her some help."

"I need to stay away from her," Tony volunteered. "I've got my own drug issues and I can use that as an excuse. We've been feeding off each other. In enabling her, she's enabling me. Lily's pretty messed up and that's opened my eyes to what I've been doing to myself as well as to her."

"Thank you, Tony, for your frankness," Benjamin said. "We'll help you as much as we can as well. I hope that in seeing the battle you're facing and acknowledging that you have a problem will be the start on your road to recovery. Please do not hesitate to come to us with anything. You know that, don't you Son?"

"Yeah, I do. Thanks."

Rex spoke up. "I feel sort of responsible for Lily. I'm the one that brought her into our family and I feel like I should be the one to help her."

Mike immediately interrupted. "No! I don't think you or I are the one to do this. It's too close to us."

"Then who better to help her?" Rex answered. "You don't need to feel responsible. I understand where she is. I don't understand why yet, but I believe that I can help her. I'm not a partier. I can get to know her better, spend some time with her, and talk to her. If I get her to trust me and open up to me, I just may be able to save her."

Benjamin went over and rested his hand on Rex's shoulder. "I think Mike may be right on this one, Rex. Your judgment may be clouded. You both have too much of a personal connection to this."

"Which is why I should be the one to do this," Rex argued. "Please. You have to let me try. If I get in over my head, I'll come to you for help. I have to do this, not for me or anyone else. I need to do this for Lily."

After a few hours of discussions, they finally decided that Tony would no longer spend time with Lily. He did insist that he continue to supply her for her needs so he could control what she was getting and how much. Rex would take over picking her up and taking her home. If she had less time alone, she may use less. If a friendship developed, he may be able to piece together her past situation that got her into this problem. It may have been as simple as being at the wrong party with the wrong people when she was younger. He had seen that before. The guys were right about one thing though. This was very personal to Rex and Mike and they understood what she was going through better than anyone else was in that room.

As rehearsals and concerts resumed, Tony informed Lily that he had some personal issues and he wouldn't be able to drive her anymore. He told her that Rex was willing and available to act as her personal chauffer. Lily was agreeable to this change although she knew it meant the end of their partying. She knew that Rex wasn't someone that would condone that type of behavior.

As spring continued, Lily and Rex had fallen into a routine that was comfortable. A friendship was even beginning to develop although Rex didn't ask questions that were too personal. Lily never discussed herself but asked a lot about Pam's business. She had a natural flare for interior decorating as well and was very interested in Pam's talents and clients.

Rex owned a convertible sports car and as soon as the evenings were warm enough, he asked Lily if she wanted the roof down. She was thrilled to feel the wind in her hair and the illusion of the freedom of flying. Unfortunately, she was still drinking heavily and her ever-present bottle of Cola always contained more than soda pop. Rex couldn't control what she did when she was at home alone, but he made her aware of how many pills she was taking. Often she wouldn't remember that she had already taken some and he had to stop her by reminding her.

This situation was quite stressful for Rex. It had been a long time since he was responsible for anyone. Even his own wife wasn't dependant on him. He didn't feel like he was making any progress with Lily, but he knew it was going to be a long and slow process.

On one particularly warm night, Rex was driving Lily home after a concert. It was very late and he had the roof down. They laughed and sang all the way to Lily's house. When he pulled into her driveway, he turned off the engine. They sat in silence and Lily had her head tilted back against the headrest and stared into the sky.

"You know what I miss about living in the country?" Lily asked.

"The smell of cows?" Rex laughed.

Lily giggled. "No. I miss the stars."

"There are stars up there. I see lots." Rex also tilted his head back to gaze into the sky.

"You can see so many more stars in the sky away from the city lights. On a clear night, you can even see The Milky Way. Have you ever been up north? Have you ever been in Canada?"

"I've done some shows in Vancouver, Toronto and Montreal," Rex answered.

"I mean further north, away from big cities."

"No, I haven't had the pleasure."

"We used to sit out at night and watch the Northern Lights. It's the most amazing and beautiful thing I've ever seen. Solar particles colliding with gases in our atmosphere cause it. Very scientific, but it creates such a sense of awe. It's incredible."

"You sound homesick," Rex fished. "Did you grow up in Canada?"

"That was another life." Lily sighed. "I'm tired. Thanks again for the ride."

Lily started to get out, but Rex wanted to keep her talking. He thought a door might have opened and he wanted to take advantage of the opportunity to talk about her past.

"Can I come in?"

"It's awfully late, Rex."

"I know. It's just that Pam's away again and I'd like someone to talk to for a few minutes."

Lily hesitated then smiled.

"Sure. You are more than welcome to come in."

Rex raised the roof of his convertible while Lily fumbled in her purse for her keys. Rex grabbed her bags for her as she unlocked the door.

Jackson came to greet Lily and she picked him up. She buried her face into his neck and murmured to him.

"How's Mama's baby? Have you been waiting for me? I'll bet you want your night time snack."

Rex was amused in the way that Lily spoke in cute baby talk to her cat. It was a relaxed, vulnerable side of her that she hadn't shown before.

"Make yourself comfortable in the living room. I'm going to get Jackson something to eat. Do you want something to eat? I'm hungry myself."

"No, I'm fine thanks."

"What about a drink? Do you want a beer?"

"Sure."

Lily opened a can of cat food for Jackson and got some potato chips and the beer. She joined Rex on the sofa.

"What would you like to talk about?" Lily asked while munching.

"Well," Rex stammered, "I don't know. I just wanted some company."

"Where's Pam this week?"

"She's in New York City. Last week she was in Los Angeles and the week before that it was London, England."

"She's traveling more than you are. What does she do on these trips?"

"She buys antiques and furniture and knickknacks for her clients. I didn't realize that someone had to travel so far to get specific items for certain designs."

"There's a lot about interior decorating common folk don't understand," Lily jibed.

"I'm beginning to realize how our wives feel when we go away and leave them behind."

"You need a cat. They're great companions."

Almost on cue, Jackson trotted into the living room and jumped into Lily's lap. He looked at Rex and meowed loudly.

"Jackson has been my faithful companion, my friend and my confidante." She petted him until he curled up in her lap and fell asleep, purring loudly.

"Why are you alone?"

"It's easier that way. I don't have to answer to anyone and I can do as I please. Besides, I have enough problems that I need to deal with without having someone adding to them."

"You sound bitter."

Lily shrugged and continued to stroke Jackson's fur.

Rex continued, "It sounds like you've been hurt."

"Hasn't everyone? I don't want to talk about it."

"All right, But if you ever want to, I'm here for you."

Lily looked up at Rex. "You mean that?"

"Yes, I do." Rex reached over and picked up her hand. "I want to be your friend. I care about you and it hurts me to see you so lonely. I want to help."

"Thanks, Rex, but I'm pretty messed up. I'm not someone that people can befriend. Besides, I'm not lonely with Jackson."

"I think you have a beautiful personality. You're friendly and charming and you have a great sense of humor."

"I have an ugly past. I'm not someone you'd want to know."

"Actually, I do."

Lily pulled her hand out of Rex's. "It's late. I'm tired. I'm not prepared or willing to have this conversation right now."

"I just want you to know that I care and that you can trust me."

"Trust is not something that comes easily to me."

"I know that. That's why I'm reaching out to you. Take your time. I don't want to rush you, but I promise you that if you ever do feel the need to talk, I'll be there. I also promise you that I will keep in the strictest confidence anything I learn about you. I will never betray you. Never."

"Right now, I just want to go to sleep. I don't want to be rude, but it's time you went home."

"Ok. Don't get up. Jackson looks too comfortable. I'll show myself out."

Rex stood up but then leaned over and kissed Lily on the forehead. "Good night."

Chapter Nine

Over the next month, Rex drove Lily to and from concerts and rehearsals. He didn't ask to come into her house again. He thought it was too soon. He didn't want her to feel threatened and scare her away. He wanted to win her trust and open up to him on her own terms and in her own time. She spoke more freely each night they drove home.

Rex was thankful for the warm spring nights and summer was very near. Lily seemed much more comfortable and confident when the roof was down on the car. Rex was trying to stick with his plan to get Lily to talk about her life. He sensed that there were some very ugly monsters in her past. Those drove her to drink and use drugs so much. Quite possibly, the headaches were a manifestation of all she endured and kept hidden. If only he could discover them, he hoped that it would begin the healing process for her.

Threshold was upon a scheduled break in their routine. They planned the break early on to avoid burnouts and frustrations that inevitably happened when a large group of individuals spend so much time together. Rex was worried about Lily being alone knowing he was going away for the break. He wished that he could cancel his trip with Pam, but they had planned it together over a year ago. The night of the last concert before the summer break was a warm, clear night.

To celebrate the break, Threshold threw a party after the concert. There were lots of drinks and some drugs going around. This was not something they normally did, but every now and then, a good party was enjoyed. It was getting quite late and Rex needed to get home, so he left with Lily to drive her home first. Once again, the roof was down on the car as they drove to her house. He hoped that he would not be stopped by police since he knew he was well over the legal limit.

"It's so nice tonight," Rex said.

"Yeah," Lily sighed. "Springtime seems to be the toughest time of year to get through. That transitional period seems to be so rainy and gloomy. It's depressing."

"Ah, but springtime is a time of re-birth. The flowers start to bloom. The leaves start to bud. Birds build their nests."

"Weeds start to grow. Spiders start to build their webs. Mosquitoes start to bite," continued Lily.

"For such a beautiful woman, you certainly have a pessimistic outlook on things."

"Welcome to my life."

"Would you like to go for a walk somewhere?" Rex asked.

"At this hour?" asked Lily. She paused for a moment. "Oh, sure. Why not? Jackson won't starve."

Rex parked the car and put up the roof. They got out, both a little unsteady on their feet and began to walk.

"It's such a beautiful night," Rex explained. "Is there a better way to enjoy a night like this than to walk with a beautiful woman by my side?"

Rex offered his arm to Lily and she giggled as she slid her hand through his arm. They walked aimlessly and silently for awhile. They came upon a park and they ended up by the swings. Lily detached herself from Rex and sat on one of the swings. Rex sat on the swing next to her and watched as she started to swing. She went higher and higher and he worried that she might fall. She soon dragged her feet to stop. They sat in silence.

"Rex?" Lily asked.

"Yes?" Rex answered.

"You told me twice tonight that I was beautiful."

"Only twice? It should have been more."

Lily looked at him. Her face was shadowed so he couldn't see her expression. Rex felt more at ease and artificially emboldened.

He continued, "Lily, it's no secret that we all think that you are beautiful. You have an amazing voice and an incredible presence that cannot be ignored or denied."

Lily looked away. "I guess I don't see myself as others do. I find it hard to accept compliments."

"You should get used to it."

Rex got off the swing and stood in front of Lily. He put his hands out and she took them as he helped her up. They stood facing each other and continued to hold hands.

"I can feel something developing between us. I want to remind you that I'm here for you. If you ever want to talk or just be with someone, call me. You have my cell phone number. Just dial and I'll be there as soon as it's humanly possible."

A cool breeze blew suddenly, making Lily shiver.

"I left my jacket in the car. Can you take me home now?"

Rex put his arm around Lily's shoulder and walked her back to the car. He began to drive her home again, but now the roof was up and Lily was very quiet. Clouds quickly covered the sky and by the time they arrived at Lily's house, it was raining.

"Is Pam away again?" Lily asked.

"She's in Paris, France this week," Rex answered.

"Is she ever home?"

"Not much anymore."

"Do you want to come in?"

"I'd love to."

Lily unlocked the door and carried on with her nightly ritual of feeding and playing with Jackson. Soon, Lily and Rex were sitting on the sofa with Jackson curled up in Lily's lap sleeping.

"How long have you had Jackson?" Rex asked.

"I've had him about five years. When I moved into this house, it was pretty big and lonely, so I got a kitten. He's been my best friend ever since. He's very loyal." Lily paused. "Can I ask you something?"

"Sure."

"Did I do something to upset Tony?"

"Not that I know of. Why?"

"He just stopped suddenly driving me home and passed me off to you. You've been great company. It was just so sudden."

"Tony has some personal issues that he's trying to work out. I think he was worried that he'd drag you down with him."

"Do you know what his problems are?"

"I have an idea, but I wouldn't be much of a friend if I spoke about it, would I?"

Lily was petting Jackson, but she was not relaxed any more. She worried that Tony would drop out of her life completely. So far, he was continuing to pick drugs up for her, but she worried that she would be cut off and wasn't sure how she would find a new source again. Rex noticed her sudden agitation and nervousness.

"Are you all right?"

"No. I'm just really uptight."

"Is there anything I can do to help?"

"Yes. I mean no."

"Which is it? I'll leave if you want me to, but I'd rather stay and make sure you're all right."

"I enjoy your company. Really I do. It's just that, well, I need to do something."

"Go ahead."

"I need a joint. I need one to help me unwind." Lily paused. "I guess I shouldn't have just blurted it out like that. I like to wind down before I go to sleep. Pot helps me relax. I'm sorry if I offend you."

"You don't offend me. This may surprise you, but nothing surprises me about you."

"Am I that transparent?"

"No, you're anything but transparent. I would love for you to open up and tell me all about yourself. Maybe some day you'll trust me enough to do that. I just mean that I have personal experience with some of your habits and I recognize all the signs of all the drinking and drugs that you do. I hope I don't offend you."

"No, I guess I don't hide my use very well. I was just afraid that if I was upfront about it, you guys would never have given me a chance."

"I hate to tell you this, but you haven't fooled anyone. Everyone's worried about you, but we all agreed to stay out of your business, so we'd never bring it up if you didn't."

"Do you still use?"

"Very rarely."

"Maybe you should leave then."

Rex felt confused. He felt that the door had finally opened and she was starting to open up. If he left, she might never get close to him again, feeling that he had walked away from her because of her problems. If he stayed, he would be saying that it was all right and acceptable for her to continue to abuse her body with drugs. He needed to let her know that he was on her side somehow and that he understood her. That he accepted her so she would trust him further. Already influenced by the alcohol he had consumed earlier, he made a decision.

"I'll join you," Rex blurted out.

Rex was just as surprised at his comment as Lily was.

Chapter Ten

Lily shooed Jackson off her lap and stood up.

"Come with me," she said to Rex.

Rex followed Lily up the stairs. Lily had eloquently decorated the upstairs as well. All rooms had oak hardwood floors, area rugs, oak window blinds and sage green window dressings. There were four bedrooms upstairs, although one contained boxes and bins stacked neatly. One smaller room was furnished as a guest room while another had a keyboard and other musical accoutrements. The master bedroom was obviously the one Lily used. Both the hallway and the master bedroom connected the upstairs bathroom.

"My house has a secret," Lily said. "You have to promise not to tell anyone about it."

"All right, I promise."

Lily went into her bedroom and opened the double doors to the walk-in closet. Clothes hung neatly inside. She stepped into the closet and called Rex after her. As he stepped into the closet after her, Lily had already pushed the clothes to one side and was pushing the back wall of the closet, which turned out to be a sliding pocket door. She stepped through and flicked on a light switch. A beautiful loft was softly illuminated. Fans were set into the walls to circulate the air since there were no windows.

"I don't think Jackson even knows about this room. This is my secret hide-away," Lily explained. "I love to come up here to relax, especially when it's raining."

The patter of raindrops hitting the roof was very soothing and melodic.

"This is the space above the garage," Rex observed.

"Yes. Clever isn't it? I know a guy, Shawn, in Toronto who is a very good contractor. He's not licensed to work in the States, but he came down and did me a favor. He refinished the entire house and built this for me. He even put some final decorating touches through the whole house."

Rex looked around the loft. It wasn't large, but it was a good size room. Lily had a matching sofa and chair in the sage green she obviously loved so much. The floor was oak as well as the matching tables that adorned the room. A beige area rug made the floor warm on the feet.

For the first time, Rex noticed several canvases and easels set up with oil paintings in various stages of completion.

"Wow! You paint too?" Rex marveled. "Is there a talent you don't have?"

"I just dabble," Lily answered.

"These are very good. Have you considered selling them?"

"I have given a few away and Shawn comes down every once in a while to gather a few for some of his clients. He pays me well."

"I'm very impressed. Pam would love to get her hands on these."

Rex looked at the signatures on the finished pieces. The same initials of D.M.E. were on these as the ones downstairs.

"Those are your paintings in the living room!"

While Rex admired her artwork, Lily went to a small stereo system and put on a CD. Quiet jazz music filled the loft. She then went to another painting on the wall that turned out to be hiding a safe behind it.

"Your Canadian friend thought of everything."

Rex continued to enjoy her paintings while Lily rolled some joints. She sat on the sofa and patted the seat next to her. Rex joined her but felt nervous. He was convinced he was doing all the wrong things. He was supposed to be getting her to trust him so he could help her stop using and all he was doing was joining her. If he left, Lily would just continue what she was doing but she would be alone. Another part of him really wanted to do this with her.

Rex was uncertain as to what to do. She lit the cigarette and inhaled deeply. She closed her eyes and immediately looked at peace. Her eyes still closed, she handed the cigarette to Rex. He took it but then hesitated before inhaling. It really had been years since he did any drugs. He looked over at Lily who was lying back against the couch with her eyes still closed. She looked more at peace than he had ever seen her. She was so incredibly beautiful and looked so vulnerable.

Rex inhaled and handed it back to Lily. He had to touch her arm before she took it. They continued to smoke more joints and listen to the rain and the jazz. Rex remembered how incredible this made him feel. In combination with his earlier drinks, all his senses heightened. The sounds were clearer, colors were brighter and touch was so much more sensitive. Lily smiled at him and he couldn't resist her.

"You are the most incredibly beautiful woman I've ever met. The moment I laid my eyes on you at Bobbi-Jo's that first night; I knew you were someone special. I had to know you. Then when I heard you, I knew you were what Threshold was looking for. That was such a thrill because it meant that I had a chance to have you in my life in some capacity. I fell in love with you the moment I saw you and my feelings for you have only grown. I need you in my life."

Lily snuffed her cigarette out in an ashtray then stood up and turned to Rex.

"Rex, you're not sober right now. Please don't say or do anything that you're going to regret later."

Rex stood up also and reached for Lily's hands.

"My only regret is that I didn't have the courage to say this to you when I was sober. I know exactly how I feel and what I'm doing."

Lily pulled away from him.

"You don't know me."

"I want to know you. I want to know everything about you. What I do know, I love."

"You have no idea who I am. You have no idea what I am."

"I know that you are a very beautiful woman who is talented in so many ways. Everything you do has a touch of gold to it. You have a warm and caring personality, even if you hide yourself away with the booze and the drugs. There's a lot of depth to you and I can see it. I can feel it."

"I'm not real! I'm only a façade! Lily Rose Delphinium does not even exist!"

Rex moved to her and held her in his arms.

"This woman that I'm holding is very real. I want to be with you. I don't care about the past. I don't care about the future. I only care about right now. Lily, please. I want you."

Rex began to kiss Lily. At first, she resisted but then she began to respond.

"Rex…" Lily began. Then she returned his kiss deeply. She whispered, "I want you too."

Lily pulled away and led Rex back to her bedroom. He began to unbutton her blouse and he continued to kiss her ears, her neck and her shoulder. She closed her eyes and for the first time in her life, was enjoying the sensations that someone could cause her to feel.

"Dora," Lily whispered.

"What?"

"My name," Lily explained, "is Dora. Please call me Dora when you make love to me."

After they spent their passion, Lily fell asleep with her head on Rex's chest and her arm draped across him. He stroked her shoulder and realized that during the entire time that he knew her, he had never seen her arms. She always wore long sleeves in blouses and sweaters. As she slept, he ran his fingers down the length of her arm. There was enough light to admire her well toned muscles and milky white skin. He thought he noticed some scaring so he studied her arm. At closer scrutiny, he could see that the scars were old needle marks. They had healed over, but there were a lot of them.

Rex felt a sudden panic. The effects of the marijuana had worn off and he recognized how careless he had been. Lily had tried to warn him off. If intravenous drug use was a part of her past, there was a real possibility that she could be HIV positive. She certainly had issues that caused her to lose herself in a constant chemical haze. Rex was no closer to discovering what they were. The booze and marijuana had caused him to completely lose control and only now acknowledged that he had been in denial about his feelings for this woman he hardly knew.

Lily stirred in her sleep and turned over, facing away from Rex. He held her from behind as she slept. She looked very peaceful and happy. Despite his concerns, Rex was still bursting with love for her and seeing her so relaxed filled him with a sense of pride. Lily slept soundly and he began to brush her hair back away from her face and shoulder. That was when he noticed more scars. He pulled her hair back very gently so as not to disturb her, but he revealed her head, neck and back. He was horrified to see such ugly scars.

One scar was over five inches long and it began beneath Lily's right shoulder blade and ran jaggedly down at an angle to her ribcage. Bad scars also covered the back of her skull behind her right ear. It was no wonder that she suffered from headaches if she had received an injury that left scars of that magnitude.

Lily had told Rex that she had an ugly past. He hadn't doubted her, but seeing those scars made the fact tangible. Lily had definitely been the victim of some serious brutality. He began to understand more completely, why she would hide from reality and mistrust people. He understood her need to dull the pain, both physical and mental and to escape whatever bitter memories haunted her every waking moment.

Lily would have to deal with her past and somehow conquer it. She may be able to fight it with proper counseling and rehabilitation. Rex held her close and fought back the tears that stung his eyes. All he wanted to do now was protect her from further harm and make her well.

"My darling," whispered Rex, "what has happened to you? Did I just make things better or worse for you?"

Rex became aware of the time. He knew that in a few short hours, Pam would be phoning from France as prearranged. He had to be home but he could not tear himself away from Lily. He had not planned for any of this to happen. He had betrayed his wife and didn't know what to do next.

Lily stirred and turned over. She opened her eyes and smiled sleepily at Rex. "Hi."

Rex smiled back at her. "Hi. Are you all right?"

"I've never felt better. You are very sweet."

Rex began to kiss Lily, but she put her hands on his strong chest and pushed him back a bit.

"You need to go home."

"I don't want to leave." Rex began to kiss her again. "I'm afraid that if I leave, I'll lose you. I don't ever want this moment to end."

"We both know that you can't stay. I don't want to kick you out, but you need to go home."

Rex closed his eyes and nodded. Once again, he felt the bitter sting of tears against his eyelids.

"Hey," whispered Lily, "it's all right. You know where to find me. I'm not going anywhere. We're friends, remember?" She reached up and wiped away a tear that trickled down his cheek.

"I didn't mean to hurt you."

Lily propped herself up on her elbow while pulling the sheet over her chest. "Do I look hurt? I'm fine. I feel terrific. What happened between us means a lot to me. You mean a lot to me. Therefore, you need to go home and get some sleep."

Rex once again kissed Lily deeply. "Can I call you later?"

Lily smiled. "Of course."

Rex dressed and reluctantly left Lily snuggled in her warm bed. He let himself out and unlocked his car. As he drove home, he was not pleased with himself. He should have been stronger and resisted his attraction to Lily. He had been in denial since the moment he first saw her. He should never have allowed himself to weaken and smoke the marijuana and that triggered the release of his forbidden feelings for her. He had been completely out of control. Now he crossed a boundary and still didn't know what he was going to do next. He broke through Lily's defenses but at what cost? He was concerned that he would make matters worse for her. He had no choice but to pull back. He was afraid that if she felt used, she might fall deeper in her despair. He should not have left her alone so soon after he made love to her. He was supposed to be going home to get some sleep before Pam phoned. He knew, however, that he wasn't going to get much sleep at all.

Chapter Eleven

Rex had just managed to fall asleep when the ringing of the phone startled him awake. It was nine o'clock in the morning as scheduled. Confused, it took him a few seconds to clear his head and remember where he was. He answered and heard Pam's cheerful voice. She discussed her trip and the purchases she was making. She was always very excited and seemed much happier when she took these trips. They confirmed her arrival home in two days. Their planned vacation to Colorado would go ahead on time.

"Is everything all right there?" Pam asked. "You sound tired."

"I am tired."

"Didn't you sleep well? Do you miss me after all?"

Rex needed to get his emotions under control. He decided to reveal a portion of the truth to explain the situation but the whole truth would have to remain buried deep within it.

"I have a confession."

"Oh?" Pam sounded concerned.

"It's Lily. She's pretty sick."

"Oh, no! What's wrong?"

"I promised her that I wouldn't divulge any information, but I'm pretty wrapped up in this so you're going to need to know what's going on."

"I'm listening," Pam said.

"Her substance abuse is out of control. She's an alcoholic and a drug addict."

For a while, there was nothing but silence on the other end of the line.

"Are you still there?"

"I'm here," Pam paused. "Why didn't you tell me this before?"

"I made a promise to her."

"Does everyone know?"

"Everyone in the band knows. I don't know how much the general public knows, but they must be aware."

"I get the feeling that you're not telling me the whole truth."

"I've taken on the responsibility to help her."

"Rex, no!" Pam exclaimed over the phone. "You can't do this again. It tore you apart the last time. This time you may lose your sanity completely!"

"I can help her. I know I can. She came into our lives for a reason. You're the one who found her and I'm the one that brought her into this family. She's one of ours now and she needs my help."

"You can't save her."

"I have to try!"

"She's not family!"

"She is part of this family."

"She's not your sister! You can't bring Rachael back by trying to save Lily!"

"I couldn't save Rachael but I have a chance to save Lily. I need the chance. I need to try."

Rex could hear Pam sigh heavily across the miles.

"I'll be home in two days. We'll continue this discussion then."

"There's nothing more to discuss. I need to do this. I need to do whatever it takes to save Lily and I need to have your support behind me."

"You're going to do this with or without my support," Pam said. "I'll call you tomorrow at the same time."

With that, the line went dead. Rex hung up and ran his fingers through his hair. For the first time in years, he offered up a prayer. He was in over his head and he felt that it wouldn't hurt to ask for some divine intervention.

When Rex awoke again, it was almost two o'clock in the afternoon. He reached over to the bedside phone and dialed Lily's number. There was no answer. He had a quick shower then tried to phone Lily again. There was still no answer. He ate a breakfast of toast and orange juice then tried to phone Lily once more. Yet again, there was no answer. He became worried and decided to drive over to her house to see if she was all right.

Once Rex arrived and parked in her driveway, he went to her front door. Frustrated by the fact that she had no doorbells, he knocked loudly. He wondered how Lily's contractor friend could overlook doorbells and decided that he would install them himself after he returned from Colorado. Rex knocked loudly again and called her name.

"What's the emergency?" Lily asked as she rounded the corner of her house. She was wearing a sunhat and garden gloves while holding a trowel. She had a smudge of dirt on her cheek under her right eye.

"Lily!" Rex sighed with relief. "I tried phoning several times and when you didn't answer, I got worried, so I came over to see if you were all right."

"Of course I'm all right. Why wouldn't I be? I've been preparing my flowerbeds all day. I don't hear the phone when I'm outside and I don't like being captive to it by carrying around the cordless." Lily paused. "Would you like to come in where it's cooler?"

"Sure. Thanks."

They went in through the back door and went to the kitchen.

"Would you like a beer?" Lily asked.

"No, thank you."

"How about Iced Tea?"

"That sounds good. Thanks."

"Make yourself comfortable in the living room. I have the air conditioner on in there. I'll bring the drinks."

Rex sat on the leather sofa, admiring once again the softness and quality of it. He felt nervous and began to wring his hands. Jackson jumped up onto his lap and began to rub his head against Rex's hands. Lily followed shortly with the drinks. She handed him his Iced Tea while she sipped her cold beer from the bottle.

"Thank you," Rex said.

"Jackson's taken a liking to you." Lily sat next to him and put her bare feet up on the coffee table. She had shed her muddy shoes and Rex felt foolish for not doing the same.

"Should I take my shoes off?"

"No, they're fine." Lily took another drink. "So, why were you so worried about me that you had to rush over here?"

"I guess I just overreacted. I thought maybe you were hurt or something."

Lily laughed. "That's sweet of you, but I've been taking care of myself long before I ever met you." She raised her bottle and looked at it. "I may not have done the greatest job, but I'm still here."

"What are your plans over the next few weeks?"

"I'm planning to finally get my flower gardens done. I'm quite a bit behind this year. I'm also going to trim my hedges and clean up the yard, clean out the shed and garage and paint the fence. I'm also planning to give this house a thorough cleaning. When do you leave for Colorado?"

"Pam's due back the day after tomorrow. We'll be leaving after that." Rex played with his glass. "Lily. Or should I say 'Dora'? What do I call you?"

Lily smiled. "Call me Lily. That's who I am now."

"All right. Lily, don't you have somewhere to go? You mentioned living in Canada before. Do you still have family there?"

"No."

"Where is your family?"

"Dead." Lily took another drink.

"All of them?" asked Rex.

"All of them," repeated Lily.

"I'm so sorry. What happened?"

"Maybe another time."

"All right."

There was a long silence between them. Lily drank her beer and Rex played with his glass.

"Can we talk about last night?"

"Sure."

"Usually two people get to know each other a little better before they sleep with each other."

"Not always."

"I feel that at least some questions should have been asked."

"What sort of questions?"

"Well, I can tell you that I'm in perfect health. I don't have any nasty diseases or anything and I should have let you know that before we did what we did."

"And you need to know about me."

"I'm sorry. I don't mean to be rude. I feel that I pushed you after you initially resisted."

"You have regrets." It was a statement, not a question.

"Actually, no, I have no regrets at all. I just think we should have discussed a few things first."

Lily put her beer down on the coffee table. She turned to face Rex.

"I'm fine. I would never do anything to hurt you. I was tested for everything a few years back and I'm fine." Lily paused. "In case you're wondering, I haven't been with anyone else since then."

There was an awkward silence for a few minutes.

"What happens now? Where do we go from here?"

Lily smiled and stroked his cheek. He hadn't shaved yet.

"We continue to build the friendship that we've started." Lily said. "Last night was what it was. It was great. It was wonderful. You were so sweet. However, you don't owe me anything and I don't want to have to owe you anything. I care about you, but I don't have the strength right now to have the kind of relationship that we would have to have."

"I don't want what happened between us last night to hinder our friendship," Rex said. "I can't help but feel that I pushed things too far and too fast."

"Nothing happened that I didn't want to happen. It's something between us that we don't need to reveal to anyone else. It was only sex. It may even make our friendship stronger."

Rex reached out and put his free arm around Lily. She leaned into him and rested her head on his chest.

Rex said, "I said a lot of things last night. I have to be completely honest with you. I meant every word that I said." Lily looked up at him and smiled. Rex continued, "I do love you. I just need to learn how to channel that emotion into our friendship."

"You are sweet. Everything's all right between us. Do you trust me?"

"Of course. I think I proved last night that I'd trust you with my life."

"Good. Now leave. I need to get back to my weed garden so I can find some flowers."

Rex smiled and got up to leave. Lily put her sandals on and walked him to his car.

"You stay safe and have a good time in Colorado."

"Thanks. If you need anything at all, call Mike or Andy. They'll be close by. Maybe even give Cindy a call. She doesn't get out much with Kevin and she'd probably enjoy some adult company."

"Please stop worrying about me," Lily complained. "I'll be fine."

With a reassuring smile from Lily, Rex got into his car. He waved and started it. As he backed out, he looked at Lily who was standing in the driveway with her hands on her hips. He waved again and she waved back. She headed for the backyard as he drove off towards his home. They may have talked things over but he felt like there was a lot of unfinished business left between them.

Chapter Twelve

The summer weeks went by quickly and Threshold's schedule began to get busy. Over the next few months, they would still be playing close to the Chicago area but then they were going to start on a cross-country tour. They were going to begin in Vancouver, Canada and work their way across the United States with three more dates in Canada. Everyone in the band was concerned about Lily. Lily was concerned about her supply of drugs. Cindy and Kevin were going to keep Jackson while she was gone.

Threshold was working several days of rehearsals to revamp the old material and to work on some new songs that Mike had written. Rex hadn't been doing much writing lately but Mike kept busy with his songs. During an afternoon rehearsal at Beady Eye's sound stage, two men dressed in dark suits arrived. Benjamin spotted these men and approached them.

"Howdy, Gentlemen. My name is Dapril. I own this place. How can I help you?"

The taller man spoke, "We need to speak with Miss Delphinium."

"She's in the middle of rehearsal right now. We can schedule an appointment for you later in the week."

The tall man took out his wallet and flashed an F.B.I. badge.

"We need to speak with Miss Delphinium," he repeated.

"All right." Benjamin went over to the sound booth and pressed a button. He spoke into a microphone and his voice boomed over the stage monitors.

"Take five, guys."

The band stopped mid-song.

"Lily and Rex come here please," Benjamin commanded.

Lily and Rex looked at each other as they left the stage.

"Do you have any idea what this is about?" Rex asked Lily.

"No. I was hoping you knew."

"What's up?" asked Rex when they reached the three men. Lily blanched when she saw the agents but kept quiet.

"These men are here to speak to Lily. They're with the F.B.I."

Benjamin turned to the agents.

"Rex Landers is our official representative and no one speaks to anyone in our organization without him present at all times."

"Not this time," the tall agent said.

"Then you can't speak to Lily," said Benjamin.

"No," Lily spoke up, "it's all right."

"Do you know these men?" Rex asked her.

"I don't know these men personally but I know what they're here to discuss with me. Is there somewhere private that we can talk?"

Benjamin escorted the group to a nearby conference room that was not in use.

"I still think I should go in there with you," Rex said.

"I'll be all right," Lily reassured him with a smile.

"I'll be waiting right here. Just come and get me if you need me."

"Thank you."

As Lily closed the door Rex heard one of the agents say, "You've got yourself a pretty good gig here. It's too bad it's going to cost you so much."

Rex hovered outside the door trying to hear their words. He cursed the building designer for doing such a good job soundproofing these rooms. He caught a few words once in awhile spoken loudly by the agents. He never heard Lily however.

"...crazy stunt..."

"...no more money..."

"...no longer protect you..."

The rest of Threshold came out to join Rex after Benjamin went back to the sound stage and told them that he thought Lily might be in trouble with the Feds. After twenty minutes, the door opened. The two agents left without a word. Lily was sitting at the conference table with her head in her hands. They all went in and Rex sat beside her. He put his hand on her shoulder and she reached up and put her hand on top of his.

"Are you all right?" Rex asked.

"No. I have a headache. I need a pill and something to drink."

"Let's hold off on that for a moment shall we? Please talk to me. Tell me what's going on."

Lily looked up at him and at her new family surrounding her. A tear trickled down her cheek. She turned back to Rex.

"Take me home."

During the drive to her house, Lily remained quiet. Once there, she did not wait for Rex, but went in and straight upstairs to her loft. When Rex joined her, she was rolling a joint.

"Do you really need to do that?" Rex asked.

Lily didn't answer. Instead, she lit it and inhaled. She sat down on the sofa and held the cigarette out to Rex.

"No, thank you. What's going on?"

Rex sat next to Lily on her sofa. Her insistence on smoking the joint was to calm her down. Rex needed to remain calm and sober so he could be there to support her and listen to her. He had the feeling that she was going to open up to him and perhaps together they could begin her healing process. Jackson had found his way into the loft and sniffed around everywhere. Lily believed he was never in there before and by the manner in which he was acting, it seemed to be true. Eventually, Jackson found that it was safe and once he familiarized himself with his new surroundings, he rubbed against Rex's legs and leapt up onto Lily's lap. He proceeded to clean himself then settled down for a nap.

"My father," began Lily, "was a French Canadian. He lived in Chicoutimi, Quebec. It's a nice little place. It's a borough of another city called Saguenay. It's a good place to be from. Its claim to fame is that it has the steepest hill in Canada. Rue Dubuc has an eighteen percent grade. That's steep. I guess it's comparable to that street in San Francisco.

"Anyway, Dad was working in Milwaukee when he met and fell in love with my mother. He brought her back to Quebec when his work visa ended. They got married and a couple of years later my brother Donald was born. Three years after that, I was born.

"Dad died of cancer when I was ten years old. Mom moved back to Milwaukee with us and resettled. She never could quite get used to speaking French. I know that my English improved and my French now sucks, but Mom needed to go back home. Her parents had died years before, but the city was still home to her so she needed to be there. Three years after moving back to Milwaukee, Mom remarried. My brother, Donny, was a wild and crazy sixteen year old and was never home. We never had any idea where he was or who he was with. Mom worked a lot, so often it was just me at home after school with Willis."

"Willis is your step-father?" Rex asked.

Lily nodded. "It was shortly after I turned fourteen that he first raped me."

Rex moved to hold Lily, but she waved him back.

"Don't. Let me talk. If I stop I may not start again."

Rex sat back quietly.

"The raping went on for several months. My mother and Donny always seemed to be out. I used to try to find places to go, but Willis would find me at friends' houses and drag me home. He threatened to kill me if I ever told anyone. He would beat me but never on my face. He never left bruises that were visible.

"He discovered soon enough that I didn't put up as much of a fight if he first shot me up with heroin. Mind you, I put up a major battle the first time, but after beating me half-unconscious, he finally got the needle between my toes. After that, it wasn't long before I was addicted. By then, I would do anything with anyone to get my fix.

"I don't know how my mother never noticed what was going on. Maybe she did but chose to ignore it or live in denial. I'll never know for sure. By the time I was fifteen; Donny was eighteen and moved away to college. One day after school, Mom came home early from work. She left because she was sick and had a fever. When she got home, she found her husband in bed with her daughter.

"Mom pulled Willis off of me and started hitting and screaming at him. I was so stoned; I just laid there and watched in horror, frozen with fear. Willis hit Mom back and she fell. She got up but Willis kept beating her and ended up throwing her down the stairs. She broke her neck and died instantly.

"I vaguely remember calling the police. Medics took Mom away on a stretcher covered up with a sheet. The police arrested Willis. He was just sitting on the front steps smoking a cigarette, calmly waiting for them. They wanted to take me to the hospital but I ran and hid. I stayed home alone for several days, sick from withdrawal and sick from everything I had witnessed.

"Donny came home as soon as he could. He found me in an awful state. He panicked and derided himself for not being the man of the family and abandoning us. He said that he should have stayed around to take care of us. He did his best to get me bathed and into clean clothes. He fed me and watched over me as I slept for days on end. When I finally woke up, I was feeling weak and still felt the need for a fix, but I was alone again. I realized that it was the doorbell chiming that woke me up. To this day, I still hate doorbells.

"Police were at my door. Apparently, Donny felt he had to even the score and somehow acquired a gun. They were transferring Willis to the courthouse for his bail hearing when Donny shot and killed him. Donny was an adult now, so they tried and convicted him as one. He got twenty-five years in a maximum-security penitentiary.

"Four months into Donny's sentence, there was a brawl at the prison. Donny somehow got involved in it and someone stabbed him several times with a sharpened spoon. By the time the guards were able to clear away the prisoners and get to him, he had bled to death.

"I had no way to pay bills so the bank took the house. I was a homeless heroin addict at the age of fifteen. Along comes Ricky who took me in. At first, he just gave me a home. He fed me and gave me my fixes. Then after awhile, he said that it was time for me to repay his kindness. He let me continue to live with him, but he ended up pimping me out as his prostitute. I didn't care. I gave Ricky my money and he gave me a place to live, food to eat and heroin to shoot.

"I lived like that for two years. One night though a john was really rough with me. I've been beaten many times before, but I didn't easily recover from this one. Ricky told me that if I wasn't willing to work, I wouldn't get my fix. I rebelled. I was dying anyway. I wanted out.

"Ricky stabbed me and pulled the knife up into my back. Even the heroin didn't dull that kind of pain. After I collapsed to the floor, he hit me with something. Mercifully, I lost consciousness. That was the last thing I remembered.

"I woke up about eight months later." Lily continued. "I had had surgery to repair my crushed skull. I now have a plate back there where there used to be bone. I was free of my heroin addiction, but the doctors told me that my heart had stopped three times while they purged my body.

"The F.B.I. visited me while I was recovering in the hospital. They had arrested Ricky on other charges but they wanted to add the attempted murder of me to the list. They wanted me to testify against him. I was so confused and scared. I was having epileptic seizures because of my head injury. I had no job and no home. I had nothing to lose. In exchange, they would pay my hospital bills and set me up with a new life.

"I was guarded twenty-four/seven and was moved from safe house to safe house. One of the detectives protecting me suggested that I try marijuana because he heard that it reduced seizures better than the anti-epileptic medications. He brought me some and we used to smoke together. He never tried to seduce me. I think he genuinely cared about me. It's funny that I don't even remember his name. The seizures slowed down a lot. I continued to use the pot because of how it calmed me and made me feel. The extra bonus is that I haven't had a seizure in the past three years.

"After the trial, the F.B.I. bought me this house and paid for the renovations. I was still scared, lonely, and afraid to get close to anyone because I thought Ricky's cronies would find me. I started on the painkillers because I had terrible headaches and then I started drinking to kill the fear, the loneliness and the memories.

"And that's how Lily Rose Delphinium came to be."

Rex sat in silence, not knowing what to say or do. He knew her past was bad, but he was shocked and horrified at all that Lily had told him.

"I'm so sorry," Rex said.

He reached for Lily again and this time she fell into his arms. Jackson, disturbed from his sleep, jumped down and voiced his disapproval. He left to find somewhere else to be. Lily began to cry and Rex cried with her as he held her tight.

"I am so, so sorry," Rex repeated.

"I survived," Lily sniffed. "Don't feel badly for me. I'm sure others have gone through worse. I may be pretty messed up, but I'm alive."

"No one should ever have to endure that kind of life. You're so young and talented. You're beautiful and have a wonderful sense of humor. You have so much to give to this world."

"I've been hiding from this world for five years."

"I don't want you to hide from it anymore."

"No one else knows all of this. I've never told anyone else. I don't want anyone else to know. No one else can know."

Still holding her tightly, Rex promised Lily his confidence.

"I promise you that none of this will escape my lips. Your secrets are safe with me. I'm honored that you trust me enough to share your nightmares with."

"They shouldn't be your nightmares."

"You're not alone anymore. You now have a family that loves you and will protect you."

"The F.B.I. pulled out their support for me. They're no longer giving me money because of the public attention I've drawn to myself. I'm supposed to be hiding, not becoming famous."

"No wonder that you were so reluctant to come on board with us. Had I known, I would never have asked you. Are you in danger?"

"I honestly don't know. I'm hoping that enough time has passed and I've been forgotten."

"What happened to Ricky?"

"He got eight years."

"He could be paroled by now."

"I know. Sometimes when I'm on stage, I look out into the crowd and wonder if he's out there, watching and waiting for me."

"What about this house?"

"The F.B.I. paid for it and put it in my name. I don't have to leave it. I don't want to leave it. I love it here."

Rex and Lily sat quietly in their embrace for several minutes.

"Don't you get tired of the drugs and booze?" Rex asked. "Don't you want to stop?"

"Sometimes I do," Lily admitted. "I can feel myself dying again. I know this stuff is killing me and this time I do care. A year ago, I may not have, but now I have so much to live for. I just don't know if I can stop."

"There's a lot of professional help out there. There are great rehab facilities all over the country. Councilors can help you grieve the loss of your family, the loss of your innocence, the brutality you've faced. Only you can decide to get help for your problems. I can't do it for you, but I can be there for you every step of the way."

Rex paused. "What is your real name?"

"Dora Manon Edwards."

"That's why there's a 'D.M.E.' on all of your paintings. That's a very pretty name."

"It's not as pretty as the flowers."

"Did the F.B.I. give you the flower name?"

"No, that was my idea. They thought it was funny, so they agreed. I just thought that if I assumed a name that evoked beauty, I might feel more at peace."

"You can still achieve that peace. Together we can get there."

"Maybe someday. I don't know if I can do it just yet."

"When you're ready, I'll be here. All you have to do is ask. I'll always be close."

Chapter Thirteen

Life continued as before for Lily. Rehearsals continued and they played a few shows. Neither Lily nor Rex mentioned anything about her past. In fact, despite how close they had become, there was a defined distance between them, almost as if it was by mutual agreement. The drives in Rex's car were very quiet.

Lily appreciated the role that Rex had taken on in her life and she appreciated that he kept his promise and didn't divulge any information to anyone else. A part of her was greatly relieved to have someone with whom she could share her past. Another part of her however felt frightened, vulnerable and exposed. The intimacy she had shared with Rex, both physical and emotional was very new to her and made her uncomfortable. She wanted to believe in him and trust him. That was why she felt so afraid. She had never known anyone that she could place her trust in before.

Lily believed Rex when he told her that he never wanted to hurt her. He even said that he loved her! Not since her mother died did anyone tell her that. His professed love for her complicated matters even more. She could not allow herself to fall in love with someone she worked with. She could not allow herself to fall in love with someone that she was going to tour internationally with. She could not allow herself to fall in love with the first man she confided in. She could not allow herself to fall in love with the first man with whom she enjoyed sex. She could not allow herself to fall in love with another woman's husband.

One night after rehearsal, Rex was driving Lily home as usual. It was very quiet. Lily decided to break the silence.

"Mike and I were talking about a few changes tonight. He told me that he loved my ideas and wanted to discuss them with everyone at the next rehearsal. I just wanted to give you advanced notice."

"What changes are we discussing?" Rex asked.

"I'd love to introduce a violin into the songs. I've been concentrating on all the songs, both new and old and I think I could make it work."

"I think that might be interesting. I'd love to hear a few lines and play around with it."

"Do you think the fans would approve? We could introduce it with the newer songs early in the show and then they may be more accepting of it in the older material. It's just an idea right now. I haven't even bought a violin yet. I wanted to get your opinions and permission before adding new sounds into your band."

"First of all," Rex stated, "it's our band; yours as well as ours. Secondly, you introduced many new sounds the moment you replaced Theresa, not only with your percussion enhancements but also with your voice. Threshold fans ate you up! We probably have several more because of you. They love you. You could introduce bagpipes and a kazoo and they'd probably love that too!"

"That's giving me a lot of ideas," giggled Lily.

Rex playfully slapped her arm and they both laughed. Finally, there was a break in their discomfort with each other and very quickly, conversation began to flow again between them. The old friendship emerged as if there was never a disruption in their relationship.

As Rex rounded the corner onto Lily's street, he was startled to see the flashing lights of emergency vehicles. He was even more alarmed as he drove closer and realized that they were at Lily's house.

"Lily…," began Rex.

"I see them," Lily said quietly.

Rex pulled up to the police barricade and parked the car. As he turned off the motor, he turned to Lily.

"Wait here," he instructed her. "I'll find out what's going on and come right back."

Rex got out of his car and approached the police officers. They called another officer over and he spoke to Rex. Rex gestured towards Lily so she got out and joined them. Rex took her arm and held her close.

"This is Lily," Rex said to the officer. "She owns the house."

"What's going on?" asked Lily. "What's happened?"

"Someone vandalized your house."

"What?"

The officer began taking notes in his notebook.

"Could you please give me your full name for my files?" the officer asked Lily.

"Lily Rose Delphinium."

"I'm Officer Jay Reynolds. I am leading this investigation. Are you the sole occupant of this house?"

"Yes."

"A concerned neighbor reported some noise and some men leaving with items from your house in a blue van. Do you know anyone with a blue van?"

"No."

"Did you give permission for anyone to enter your house and remove items?"

"No."

"Can you name someone with a grudge against you? Do you owe money to anyone?"

"I don't owe any money to anyone. As for someone with a grudge, there may be someone, but as far as I know, he still may be in prison. I don't know which prison he went to."

"Can you give me the details?"

"About five years ago I testified against someone named Ricky Sinclair and he got eight years with the help of my testimony. I don't know if he is out on parole or if he's still in. The F.B.I. was in charge of that case. I don't remember any agents' names. Where's Jackson?"

"Who?"

"My cat. I have to find Jackson. He's probably scared. He might be hiding and needs me to help him. I need to find Jackson!"

Lily was starting to panic. The officer closed his notepad and put his hand on her shoulder.

"Is Jackson the only pet inside?"

"Yes! He's black and white. Have you seen him? Do you have him? Where is he?"

"I'm sorry, Miss Delphinium. Whoever did this to your house has killed your cat."

"No!" Lily whispered. She almost fell, but Rex held her tight. She was going into a state of shock.

"Get the medics over here!" Rex told Reynolds.

Reynolds called the paramedics over and they, along with Rex and Reynolds, escorted Lily to the waiting ambulance. They attached an oxygen mask over her mouth and nose and at first, she resisted.

"Ma'am, we need to put this on you and you need to breathe deeply," one of the paramedics told Lily.

They convinced Lily to leave the mask on and to sit on the stretcher. She refused to lie down. She stared lifelessly at the floor.

"Are you her husband?" the young paramedic asked Rex.

"No, but I'm the closest thing she has to next of kin."

"We'd like to give her a sedative and take her in for overnight observation."

"She's been drinking and I'm not sure if she's taken any medications or drugs this evening."

"We'll give her a mild dose and monitor her closely."

"Don't take her anywhere yet. I want to check things out and then I'll go with her."

Rex turned to Reynolds, who was still waiting next to the ambulance.

"Officer, can I walk through her house? I want to see it for myself and make note of anything that's missing and damaged."

"I can't let you touch anything until my investigative crews have gone over every inch of the house."

Rex turned back to Lily. She was unresponsive.

"Lily!" Rex shouted to her. "Lily!"

Lily still did not respond. Her eyes were glazed and vacant. Rex put his hands on either side of her face and forced her to look at him. "Dora!"

Lily's eyes finally focused on Rex. She reached up and removed the oxygen mask.

"Rex?"

"I'm right here Darling."

"He was my baby." A tear trickled down her cheek.

"I know. I'm going into your house with Officer Reynolds to check things out. I'll be right back. Do you understand me?"

Lily nodded.

"I'm not leaving you. I am coming right back. These men will take care of you. Do you understand that you are safe?"

Again, Lily nodded. Rex turned to the paramedics.

"Don't take her anywhere without me and don't leave her alone for a minute. I'm coming right back."

Once again, Rex was reluctantly leaving Lily at an inopportune moment. As Reynolds led Rex towards Lily's house, Rex took out his cellular phone and called Mike. He explained what was happening and asked him and Cora to meet them at the hospital. Mike also promised to contact the rest of the family. Rex then followed Reynolds into Lily's house through the broken patio door.

"Don't touch anything," Reynolds reminded Rex.

Rex was horrified at the damage. As they walked through each room, he noted things to Reynolds. The vandals destroyed most of the furniture by smashing or tearing it. They slashed and tore down Lily's window dressings. The cabinets were empty and walls and carpets were spray-painted. Her paintings were missing, as were all the contents of her cabinets containing her crystal and silver. They smashed her television and slashed the leather sofa. Jackson was in the upstairs bathroom. His blood covered the room. Rex felt sick and weak but he had to check on Lily's secret room.

The bedroom closet was open and they had strewn her clothes about the room, however the back wall seemed to be in place. Rex opened the pocket door and turned on the light. Reynolds looked surprised at the discovery of this room but said nothing. Whoever had done this did not know this room was here. It remained undisturbed and Rex told Reynolds so. Reynolds had a team come up and dust for prints anyway. Photographers were in every room taking many pictures from all angles. Rex needed to get Lily's insurance broker information to call them as soon as the police were done.

After he checked the whole house with Reynolds, Rex went back to the waiting ambulance. Lily lay on the stretcher with her eyes closed. The oxygen mask was in place once again.

"How is she?" Rex asked the paramedics.

"We gave her a mild sedative and she's resting. She's awake though and asking for you."

Rex entered the back of the ambulance and held her hand.

"Lily, I'm here."

Lily opened her eyes and saw Rex sitting next to her. She squeezed his hand and once again removed the mask.

"Did you see him?"

Rex nodded. "Your whole house has been wrecked. Things are destroyed and missing. I need to contact your insurance broker to get things in motion. One good thing though is they didn't find your loft. Everything's all right in there. All of your secrets are all right."

"No, they're not. I didn't stay a secret and I'm not all right."

Chapter Fourteen

The Threshold family met at the hospital to support Lily. Even most of the technical crew arrived with the notable exception of Tony. No one knew where Tony was and he was not answering his phone at home or his cellular phone. Cindy stayed at home with Kevin with strict orders given to Peter to phone her at regular intervals with any news and updates. While the doctors treated Lily for shock, Rex described the vandalism of her home, the theft of many items and the murder of Jackson.

"Lily didn't see Jackson, did she?" asked Pam.

"No. She didn't even attempt to enter her house and if she had, I would have stopped her."

"What happens now?" asked Peter.

"The police will do a thorough investigation then the insurance company will do theirs. Meanwhile, we're going to have to find a place for Lily to stay until the house gets repaired and cleaned and furniture replaced. It's going to be a big job. We'll have to hire professionals to do most of it."

Pam added, "I know her friend, Shawn. He's a busy contractor in Toronto and Lily and I talked about the work he had done on her house here several years ago. I'll call him and see if he's available to come down to help. I'm sure he'd like to do whatever he can for her.

"I'd like to redecorate the house," Pam continued. "I'll donate my time and replace the furniture. I'll do whatever it takes to get her home again."

"Beady Eye will cover all costs," Benjamin volunteered. "I'm also going to make certain she gets whatever she needs and rent her a place to live in the meantime. If I know Lily, she isn't going to like being a charity case, but she's just going to have to accept the fact that I'm the head of this family and she's a big part of it whether she likes it or not. What I say goes."

The rest of the family agreed. Each one offered to do something, regardless of how small it seemed. They all wanted the best for Lily and were willing to give of themselves for her. "She'd do it for us," they all said.

Cora interrupted, "I hate to ask, but what about Jackson? Who takes care of him? Do we know what the police protocol is? I know some people with the Crime Scene Units that clean this sort of stuff on a regular basis. I'm not saying it wouldn't bother them, but they would be professional about it. I can ask them to help."

Pam took charge of the entire project and they all continued to work out details. Doing something negated the helpless feeling they all had as they stood by while Lily suffered. After over an hour, a doctor came into the waiting room and addressed everyone.

"Are you all here on behalf of Miss Delphinium?" the doctor asked.

There was a chorus of concurrence.

"She's been stabilized, although there are further concerns. Which one of you is Rex?" he asked.

Rex stood up. "I am."

"She's asking for you."

Rex followed the doctor into the consultation room. Lily was lying in a bed with an oxygen nasal catheter and an intravenous drip in her right hand. Rex moved over to her left side and took her unburdened hand. She was very pale and beads of perspiration gleaned on her face. She smiled weakly and gently squeezed his hand.

"Hi there," Rex said softly.

"Hi," whispered Lily.

"How are you feeling?"

"I'm so tired."

"I can only imagine. You've had a pretty rough night. You should try to get some sleep."

"You don't understand," Lily sighed. "I'm so tired of living like this."

"Lily, please don't talk that way. We all need you and love you." Rex paused. "I need you and love you," he added quietly.

"I'm not suicidal. I'm quite the opposite. I told you before that I'm dying and this time I do care. I have been slowly killing myself for most of my life and I want to stop. I want to get clean but I'm scared. I haven't been sober for more than a few months total in the past seven years. I don't know how to do it and I don't know if I even can."

"That's good start," Rex reassured her. "We're all going to be here for you. You will never be alone again. We will all support you and help you in any way we can. I'm not going to lie to you. It's going to be the hardest thing you have ever done in your life, but I'm thrilled to hear you say that you want to change. You just did the biggest thing just now. I know it's cliché but admitting your problem is the first step and the most important one. It's going to get tougher, but I know you can do it. I have faith in you. I believe in you."

"Dr. Adams has been talking to me for the past half hour or so. He's the one who came out to get you. He told me about a Rehab Center that is very good here in Chicago. He wants to transfer me over there as soon as I'm ready."

"Are you all right with that?"

"I'm never going to be ready, but I don't exactly have anyplace else to go right now. I'm here now. I just don't know what's going to happen. I also don't want to let the band down."

"Don't worry about the band. Your health is the most important thing to all of us and we're all going to be behind you all the way."

"But a bunch of shows are coming up."

"We'll take things one day at a time. We can postpone until you're ready to come back."

"I don't want any commitments right now. I don't want to leave Threshold, but I just don't know what to do or how long this is going to take. I don't want to feel pressured to return before I'm ready."

"We're not going to pressure you. For now, you have a battle to fight and Threshold is going to support you, not hinder you. If you decide not to come back to the band, you'll never leave the family. You are important to us all. Together, we'll get you through this."

Rex kissed Lily's hand. "I'm very proud of you," he said.

Dr. Adams came over to check Lily's blood pressure. "I'm going to have to ask you to leave now, Sir. Miss Delphinium needs some rest."

"What happens now, Doc?" asked Rex.

"Lily and I have been discussing rather quickly her history of substance abuse. With her permission, we're going to transfer her to the Rehab Center." He turned to Lily. "You've had serious complications during your last detox, but you were also seriously injured at the time. Still, I would like to sedate you for the first few days since the initial detox stages can be tough.

"The immediate goal of detox is cleaning the poisons out of your body. We will give you detoxification medications that will suppress the withdrawal symptoms. Once we go through the withdrawal safely, we will begin the psychological readjustments. You will learn to become drug and alcohol free. You'll receive counseling both one-on-one privately with a personal therapist and you'll also participate in group counseling with others who are going through pretty much the same things you will be. It's human nature to migrate toward people with similar situations and goals, so you just might come away from this place with some new friends.

"These councilors with whom you'll be working are trained to help you repair your emotional damage and can also work with your loved ones as well. It's important for those that surround you in your life to understand what stages you're at and towards which goals you're working. During this detox period, we will give you a lot of information and assistance that will motivate you for longer-term treatments. You will work with a nutritionist to set up a healthy diet and a physiotherapist to give you exercise programs that will help you rebuild your physical body.

"Once you reach the point of being 'clean', there is going to be a whole other program to train you to live a new life so you don't relapse into old habits. There are numerous relapse preventing techniques that you will be taught.

"I know this all seems overwhelming when you're still lying here with medicines being dripped into your veins. It is a very long road to recovery and you need to understand that it's not an overnight trip. This could take months or even years and you must be committed to the entire program for you to succeed.

Part of the program is to surround you with professionals that recognize all the signs of fatigue and when you most want to quit, that's when they will push you the hardest. No one is going to give up on you and it's up to you not give up on yourself; and you will want to. This is going to be very tough, but you are young and relatively healthy and I think you'll do well."

"A lot of the current drug use started because of the pain in my head," Lily told him.

"Let's deal with one thing at a time. We'll take that into consideration and give you drug free pain reducing techniques. In the future, we may do more CT Scans of your head. We may be able to do something different to alleviate some pain. For now, however, you must say 'Good night' to your friend and you need to get to sleep." He turned to Rex. "You have two minutes."

Dr. Adams walked away and left Rex and Lily alone. She looked so frail and frightened. Rex, while still holding her hand, leaned forward and kissed her forehead.

"You're going to be safe here," Rex told Lily. "These people will take care of you. I don't want you to worry about anything other than getting well. You take as long as you need.

"You're surrounded by a lot of people who really care about you. We want you to get well. We'll take care of everything and one of us will stop by every day to check on you. If you ever need anything at all, you just have them call me or Mike or Benjamin. Someone will be here for you."

A tear trickled down Lily's cheek. Rex wiped it away and gave her a smile. He tried to let go of her hand but she squeezed tighter, looking at him with fear and sadness in her eyes.

"I won't be far. You're going to sleep now and I'll come by when they transfer you over to the Center."

"I'm scared. I don't want you to leave."

"I know. You're going to be fine. The doctor told me that I have to leave. I'll be back in a few hours. Until then, get some sleep."

Rex kissed her gently on the lips. "I love you," he whispered.

Rex left quickly before she could see his tears. He returned to the waiting family to update them on the turn of events regarding Lily's situation.

Chapter Fifteen

As promised, Rex was at the hospital for Lily's transfer to the Rehab Center. They wouldn't let him stay long with her and she was semi-conscious due to the sedating drugs. He reassured her that the family was only a phone call away and he promised to check on her every day.

After making certain that Lily was safe and comfortable, Rex hurried over to the emergency band meeting at Beady Eye. No one had been able to contact Tony, so everyone felt his absence. Everyone else sat in the conference room in a solemn mood.

"I just came from the Center," Rex updated everyone. "Lily looks pretty rough but I think she's in good hands. I would have liked to do some more research on the place, but at least she's getting the help she needs. This is not going to be quick or easy for her. We need to rally our support around her especially when it's really bad. She may reject us but we have to stand by her."

Peter spoke up, "Don't these places teach addicts to completely change their lifestyles so they don't put themselves in the same scenarios that they were in so they aren't tempted again?"

Benjamin answered, "Yes. We very well may have to face the fact that Lily might not come back to us as a part of Threshold. She may need to make a clean break of everything she knew before. We may be in the same situation as a band that we were in a year ago when Theresa left."

"I don't know about anyone else," Rex commented, "but if Lily doesn't come back, I don't think we could replace her. Personally, I don't think I could go through this again."

There were murmured agreements throughout the room.

Benjamin stood up. "I'm postponing the tour. We'll honor the ticket holders in the future. I'll have a lot to rearrange and we may not be able to postpone some shows. I've taken the liberty of talking to Theresa and she has already agreed to come on board for those shows we must do. Our fans will need some sort of explanation. I would rather not reveal the details, but there are going to be rumours and someone will reveal where she is eventually. Nothing can be kept from reporters forever."

Andy held up the local newspaper. "Front page news is Lily's home invasion. Someone even leaked the police photos onto the Web. It's a good thing Lily is out of touch. She deserves better than this."

Benjamin continued, "We need to come up with an immediate press release. I'll call for a conference tomorrow at eleven o'clock in the morning from here. We'll spend all day writing something if we have to."

Mike had been quiet during the meeting. Finally he spoke.

"Does anyone know how to reach Tony? I've been leaving messages on both his home and his cell answering systems and even sent him a bunch of emails and texts. He seems to have vanished and that has me concerned. It seems like more than a coincidence that Tony went missing at the same time as someone destroyed Lily's house. I'm worried that something may have happened to him."

Benjamin answered, "Tony admitted awhile back to having problems of his own. He may just be on a personal trip or something. We didn't need Tony for a few days so he probably isn't even aware that we're looking for him. He'll turn up eventually."

They began to work on the statement they were to release. Benjamin left periodically to tend to the tour postponement, wishing that he had an answer to the question of when they could reschedule.

The next day, Rex didn't go for his usual morning run. Instead, he drove over to the Rehab Center to check on Lily. Upon arriving, however, he met the nurse in charge of Lily's care. Her name was Bernice and she told him that Lily was in no condition to receive visitors.

"Lily is at a very crucial point in her detoxification," Bernice informed him. "She's hit a very low point and frankly, I don't think you'd want to see her in her current condition."

"I promised Lily that I'd be here for her and that I would check on her everyday. I want her to know that I'm here for her especially at the worst parts."

"I don't know if she would even know whether you were here or not. We have heavily sedated her. When she does wake up, she's very agitated and depressed. She's also in restraints."

"Restraints?" asked Rex. "Why?"

"It's for her protection. Lily has tried on three occasions to pull the I.V. out of her hand. We are concerned that she'd hurt herself so her hands have been restrained against the bed railings. There was also an incident where she punched a nurse."

Rex tried to suppress a giggle. "I'm sorry. I know it's not funny. It's just hard for me to picture that sweet-natured loving girl hitting anyone."

"Your sweet-natured loving girl is anything but that right now. Drugs change people. It's hardest when they're detoxing. The suppressed monsters have come out in full force. The patient is confused between nightmares and reality, not to mention what the withdrawal does to them. Often the patient is completely out of character. That's why I ask you to reconsider seeing her right now. She may be someone that you don't want to know at all."

"I'm willing to take that chance. I need to see her and she needs to know that I'll take the bad with the good. I will not abandon her in her worst hour. Please, let me see her."

"You've been warned."

Patients are monitored in a hospitalized setting during the detoxification period. When they have been stabilized they allow controlled visits. Once the detoxification period is over, the patient then stays in a more relaxed environment in private rooms for the duration of their stay. Celebrities are not strangers to Rehab facilities so care is always given to keep information confidential.

Bernice led Rex into Lily's room. He found himself in a darkened room that smelled terrible. He almost turned and left, thinking he was in the wrong room until he realized that the sleeping woman in the bed was in fact Lily. He almost didn't recognize her.

After only twenty-four hours, Lily still had the nasal catheter in her nose and the line in her hand had several intravenous bags attached. She was extremely thin and her cheeks had sunken in. Her skin had a grayish appearance to it and although her hair had been in a ponytail, most of it had fallen loose and hung dirtily around her face and shoulders. Traces of blood and vomit were on her hospital gown and leather straps restrained both of her wrists to each of the bedrails. Rex was appalled.

"Why is she in such a mess? Why hasn't she been cleaned up?"

"She hasn't exactly been cooperative. Maybe she'll relax with you here and we can get her cleaned up with your help."

Rex went to Lily's bedside and rested his hand on top of the restrained hand without the intravenous attached. He leaned over and kissed her forehead.

"I'm here, Darling," Rex paused.

Lily's eyelids fluttered then opened slowly. She was very groggy.

Rex spoke softly. "Hello Sleepyhead."

"Rex?" Lily whispered weakly.

"I'm here, Darling."

"Where am I? What's happening?"

"You're alright. You're in the hospital. Do you remember?"

"Why can't I move?"

"Apparently, you were trying to hurt yourself so the nurses restrained your hands. Don't struggle against them; it's for your own protection."

"I hurt so badly," Lily began to cry. "Every bit of me hurts really, really bad."

"I know," Rex said softly as he wiped her tears. He brushed her hair away from her face. "It's going to get better, I promise."

"I'm so tired and I feel so sick."

"It's the medicines they're giving you."

"What's wrong with me? Why am I here?"

"You're very, very ill. You're in the hospital getting better."

"Where's Jackson? Who's taking care of him?"

Rex remained silent, looking for an answer.

"His favorite is the tuna flavored. They've got blue labels," Lily continued. "At bedtime, I give him some chicken flavored. They have yellow labels. I leave the dry stuff in his dish throughout the day and he likes it when I mix little cheese bits in it. He loves the cheese bits."

Lily's head began to nod as she drifted back to sleep. Bernice returned with another nurse.

"Mr. Landers has offered to help us with Miss Delphinium," Bernice explained to the other nurse. "We're going to get her all cleaned up."

"Thank you. My name is Daphne," she said extending her hand.

Rex shook her hand and asked how they should proceed. Bernice removed the tubing from the intravenous catheter and unfastened the restraints. She then removed the oxygen catheter. Rex helped her lift Lily from the bed into the wheelchair that Daphne held ready.

Bernice explained, "We're short staffed right now and most of out patients are unruly. We just don't have the nurses available to help us out with cleaning them up. Our priority is getting the insides of their bodies cleaned up. It's not exactly hospital policy to allow visitors to help with the patients, especially when it involves disrobing them."

"I've seen her undressed before," Rex reassured them. "I would just appreciate it if this wasn't made known to anyone else."

"Don't worry," Bernice said, "This entire episode will be kept our secret. We could get in trouble."

Rex wheeled Lily over to the shower and Bernice and Daphne began to undress Lily. Daphne gave Rex some scrubs and he went into the washroom to change. He came out, lifted a naked Lily onto a medical chair in the shower and held her steady. She woke up and complained about being cold. Rex held her while the nurses carefully washed her hair and bathed her. She continued to complain about the cold but she didn't resist.

After Lily was clean, Bernice toweled her dry and carefully wrapped her hair with a towel. Bernice and Daphne put a clean hospital gown on her while Rex dressed. He came back and lifted her back into the wheelchair. Rex pushed her back to her bed, which Daphne had put clean linen on. He helped her back into bed and Bernice reinserted the I.V. tubing into the catheter in Lily's hand. Bernice raised the bedrails and was about to refasten the restraints but Rex stopped her.

"Let's just see how she is, alright?" Rex asked.

Bernice smiled. "I'll go and find a hairbrush." She left the room, grabbing Daphne by the hand and pulling her out behind her. This gave Rex a few appreciated minutes alone with Lily. She was groggy but was awake and looking at Rex.

"How are you feeling?" he asked her.

"Weak. Sick. In pain."

"I'm so sorry that you're going through all this but I'm here for you. I am going to take care of you. I'll start by removing the towel from your head."

Lily's wet hair draped across her shoulders. Bernice returned with a hairbrush and left it on the bedside table. Rex began to brush Lily's hair very gently.

"You're going to have to sit straight up so I can get the back," Rex instructed Lily.

Rex helped Lily to sit up and supported her with some pillows. Shortly, she began to doze again and leaned against him. Bernice came back in, took the brush from Rex and finished brushing Lily's hair. She then worked her long hair into two braids and fastened them with elastics. Rex thanked her and helped to remove the pillows and lower Lily back onto her bed. Her eyes fluttered open again.

"Rex?"

"I'm still here."

"I loved Jackson."

"I know. I did too."

"I loved Donny. I loved Mom. I loved Dad. Everyone I love dies."

"It's not your fault. You don't have any kind of power to hurt anyone by feeling something for them. You've just had a lot of unfortunate things happen in your life."

Lily looked at Rex. "I will never love you."

Rex swallowed. "You don't have to."

Lily closed her eyes. "I'm tired and I need to sleep. Thank you for all you have done for me. I do appreciate it, but don't come back."

Chapter Sixteen

The next day, Rex stopped by the hospital but Lily refused to see him. Bernice informed him that there was little change in her condition and that there may not be any for days. Rex proceeded to drive over to Beady Eye Productions for eleven o'clock in the morning. Benjamin was going to give a press conference regarding the future of Threshold and he wanted Mike and Rex to join him. There had been many rumors circulating since the vandalism of Lily's house. Some reports also suggested that a jealous lover destroyed her house and murdered Tony.

Once Rex arrived, he gave the update on Lily. At precisely eleven o'clock, Benjamin, Mike and Rex went to the conference room. Many reporters were gathered and quieted as soon as the three men entered. Benjamin stood before the microphone and cleared his throat.

"Ladies and Gentlemen," Benjamin began, "I would like to thank you all for coming this morning. I will be reading a prepared statement and will not be answering any questions at this time. All information that I currently have is in this statement. I will have no further comments after I read it.

"'On October fifteenth of this year, a crime was committed against a member of the recording group Threshold. The home of Lily Rose had been broken into and vandalized. The vandals destroyed and stole many personal items. Her pet cat had also been tortured and killed.

"'Since that time, Miss Rose has been kept in quiet seclusion. The police continue to investigate. Miss Rose wishes to re-evaluate her position with Threshold. She has not made any decisions regarding her future. We will not reveal her whereabouts. Fans may direct any communiqué or well wishes to the Beady Eye Offices.

"'The upcoming Threshold tour has been temporarily postponed. They will perform some shows as scheduled. For these events, Miss Theresa MacKenzie will return to her original role with the band. We ask all ticket holders to check with your venue in regards to cancellation notices. We request all ticket holders to keep your tickets and we will honor them at a future show in your area. If you would like to return your ticket, go to the venue or contact us for a full refund.

"'We do not know the whereabouts of Tony Sebastien nor will we comment on any speculations.'

"This ends the reading of the entire statement. Each media representative present today will receive a copy of this statement. Our website will also contain this statement. This now concludes our press conference. Thank you."

Benjamin, Mike and Rex left the room as reporters began to shout out questions. Benjamin kept his word and made no further comment.

Everything now stopped. Threshold could not move forward until Lily either rejoined the band or resigned. No one could repair Lily's house until the police completed their investigation. They could not answer any questions about Tony until they found him. For now, everyone had to wait.

Rex continued to stop at the hospital over the next week but Lily refused to see him each time. Bernice kept him updated daily and every passing day saw a slight improvement. The following week, Rex phoned the hospital instead of driving over. He asked for Bernice and waited patiently for her to come on the line. When she did, she had good news.

"Lily ate solid food this morning," Bernice informed Rex. "She ate some Jell-O and chicken broth. It wasn't much but she kept it down. That's a great sign. We've removed the oxygen and we hope to remove the I.V. in another day or so if she continues to eat. If all goes well, we'll have her on a nutritional diet and a physical exercise routine within the next two weeks. We'll start her counseling at the same time."

"What about her restraints?" Rex asked.

"Those are gone. We took them off yesterday. We sedate her less everyday and she's not violent anymore. She's being a perfect patient. We're all pleased and optimistic about her chances of a full recovery. She's very young and has a very strong survival instinct."

"Please tell her that Benjamin needs to talk to her. See if you can arrange a time that she'll agree to see him."

"Who's Benjamin?"

"He's our boss. He needs to discuss our future arrangements with her."

"Is she being fired?"

"Things must go on. He wants to reassure her that her position will be waiting for her if she wants it when she's better. He needs to keep her informed of the changes that are being made."

"I'll tell her but if she refuses to see him, we'll have to honor her request."

"I understand. Thanks for your time."

"Any time."

A few days later, Rex and Mike were working in Mike's recording studio in his house. They set up the studio years earlier and they often spent many hours working together writing and recording material. The band would hear these recordings and either dismiss or rework them until everyone was happy with it.

While Threshold was at a standstill, Benjamin arranged some recording sessions for Peter. Andy continued to work for Beady Eye's accounting department. Mike and Rex continued to get songwriters royalties and saw this unexpected break in their schedule as an opportunity to work on new material for their next

CD. With everything that had happened recently, fresh ideas were flowing and they relished the time to get these thoughts on paper and onto recordings.

As they worked through some lyrical changes, Rex's cellular phone rang. He answered to find Officer Reynolds on the other end.

"Mr. Landers?" began Reynolds. "There's been a development in Miss Delphinium's case. We've made an arrest. Actually someone has come in and confessed to being instrumental in setting up the vandalism of her home."

Rex listened for a few minutes. As the detective filled him in on the details, Rex's jaw dropped in disbelief.

....

"He turned himself in earlier this morning," Reynolds told the District Attorney. "He was extremely remorseful and confessed to being the one behind the break-in of Miss Delphinium's house.

Reynolds turned up the volume on the speaker. Another officer was speaking to a very distraught and forlorn Tony Sebastien.

"You're entitled to a lawyer to be present," the officer said.

"I waive that right," Tony answered. "I just want to make my confession to my involvement and get this over with."

The officer slid some forms across the table and handed him a pen. "Read and understand what you're signing."

After Tony signed the forms, the officer took the forms and pen. He then leaned back in his chair.

"Alright, Sebastien. Spill it."

"I swear that they were only supposed to take a few items of value. I had no idea that they were going to do the amount of damage that they did. They certainly were not supposed to hurt her cat!"

"Tell me who they are and why it's taken you so long to come forward with this."

"I only met one guy. I was coming out of my house one night a few weeks ago and he approached me. He said that he had a knife and would use it. He told me that my suppliers were unhappy with the way I was paying them and they wanted more money."

"What were your suppliers supplying you with?"

"Drugs, booze, prescription meds."

"Continue."

"This guy said that my debts would be forgiven if I gave him some more valuable information. He wanted Lily's address and schedule. I told him that I'd rather him hurt me than her. He reassured me that she wouldn't be hurt. He believed that Lily had some valuable artwork and artifacts that were worth more than my debts and they were going to go in when she wasn't at home and help themselves to a few items. I told him our schedule and gave him Lily's address and house layout. Then he told me that if I told anyone about our conversation, he would come back and use the knife on me. The night that it happened, I had gone to a friend's place in Peoria and got stoned. When I heard all that had happened I got angry then scared. I waited until I was sober to try to think of what to do. I'm really, truly scared of what this guy could do to me, but I mean, this is Lily. She didn't deserve any of this."

"I need you to write all of this down. Don't leave anything out, including a description of the man and any other information you can think of. What did he look like? What was he wearing?" The officer slid a notepad across the table. "Then, I'm going to want you to look at some pictures to try to find the man you described to us earlier. Is there anything else you want to add?"

"Only the guy's name. He said his name was Ricky."

Chapter Seventeen

By the end of November, Lily was well on her way to recovery. She was taking medication orally everyday. Her physical symptoms were no longer life threatening but she was still uncomfortable. Far worse was her emotional well-being. She had begun to see therapists on a private basis but found it difficult to reveal to them the horrors of her past.

Rex still either called or stopped by everyday, but Lily still refused to speak with him or see him. She still slept a lot and often felt weak and nauseous. She was encouraged to accept visitors on a limited basis but she was not ready to see anyone. The hospital gave Benjamin permission to bring in a few items, so he randomly brought in cards and gifts that had been arriving at Beady Eye. At first Lily objected but then reluctantly agreed. She had to admit that the well wishes of strangers, while on one level intimidating, also made her feel good that so many people cared about her. Then the demons would resurface and remind her that no one knew anything about her. She bounced back and forth between these emotions and the therapist was attempting to work with her on this.

Rex stopped by to see how Lily was. Once again she refused to see him. Rex left some fans' cards with Bernice and she brought them into Lily's room.

"You have a very dedicated young man," Bernice told Lily. "He obviously cares very much about you. He misses you."

"I don't want to see him," Lily insisted.

"He seems to feel helpless. He wants to be there for you, but there's nothing he can do."

"Don't you people teach us that we must get well on our own and for ourselves?" Lily asked. "I need to do this for myself, not Rex or the band."

"It's also important to have the love and support of people around you outside of this place. It will be someone like Rex who will continue to be with you and support you when you are in the real world. Right now, you are safe and away from all temptations. Outside, you're going to need someone that can be there for you day and night to help you through crisis times that I guarantee you will have. I can't tell you how to choose but I think he would make a very good Support Buddy.

Lily closed her eyes and lay back on her pillow.

"How do you know he isn't part of my problems?" Lily sighed. "He would probably take good care of me if he was available. I know that I can trust him but I don't want to put him at risk."

"How would you put him at risk?"

"Everyone I love dies. I can never love him."

"You don't have the personal power to make people die."

Lily opened her eyes and swung her feet over the edge of her bed.

"That's what Rex told me."

"He's a smart man."

"I can still never love him."

"I suppose it's probably best not to be in love with your Support Buddy. When there is a close personal attachment, it can get difficult. Someone that is trying to live a new life and battle with their addictions can be abusive both physically and emotionally. That can drive couples apart. However, in saying that, often the spouse or significant other has the most at stake in the relationship as long as they don't enable the addict in any way. Often, they are the most willing and available to be there. They just need to be strong. Rex seems to be very strong."

"In order for him to be available for me, either he'd have to not tour with the band or I'd have to go with them. I would never take Rex away from Threshold and I don't know if I'm willing to rejoin them on the road. I'm not sure how strong I would be. At the same time, I don't know how strong I would be at home alone in a place where so much has happened.

"Besides, I'm not so sure how his wife would feel about it," Lily added to Bernice's surprise.

By December, Lily moved into a different section of the Rehab Center. She still kept mostly to herself in a new private room. This room was similar to a motel room. Besides a hospital bed, there was a desk, chair, loveseat and coffee table. The room was also equipped with a telephone and a television. Patients were required to participate in a structured routine that forced them to interact with other patients. Breakfast was in a common eating area at seven o'clock in the morning. Exercise programs ran from eight o'clock until ten o'clock in the morning. They served lunch every day at noon. Lily had private counseling every Monday, Wednesday and Friday afternoon. Group counseling was every Tuesday, Thursday and Saturday afternoon.

Lily hated the counseling. She had a very hard time opening up about her past. Corona Towers had been counseling rehab patients for over twenty years and gave a motherly impression to those she cared for. It took awhile for Lily to trust that Corona would not run to the reporters with all of her stories. When Lily realized that didn't happen she eventually opened up during a tearful session. She wanted some form of medication to ease the psychological pain, but the nurses refused. She had to learn to deal with her past, present and future without chemical aids and it began in the safe environment of the Center.

Benjamin had a concern regarding the other patients and guests revealing Lily's whereabouts. Unfortunately, he could do little to control that. Each patient and visitor signed a privacy contract every time they left the Center that stated that any information or identities learned while there was to remain undisclosed. If someone chose to reveal that information, it would be difficult to track down the culprit. Beady Eye could not sue the Center because they had forms that patients and visitors sign to protect them from such legal action.

Many of the patients knew who Lily was. Some were enamored with her because of her celebrity status. Others seemed to hate her for the same reason. Corona tried to assist Lily with this by reminding her that they had their own issues and reasons for being in the Center and let them work out their own problems while she concentrate on hers.

Sundays were the most tedious for Lily. The chapel held an interfaith church service in the morning for anyone interested in attending. All patients were encouraged to attend, but it was not mandatory. Lily wasn't certain that she was willing to put her faith and trust in a God that had allowed all the terrible things to happen to her. She wasn't as understanding or patient as Job. She spent most Sundays watching television and sleeping.

With the holidays approaching, the decorations of various holiday celebrations began to appear throughout the Center. Staff and patients joined to decorate a Christmas tree. Christmas decorations sat among Jewish Menorahs, Dreidels, and the red, green and black colors of Kwanza and the beautifully decorated Kinaras.

Lily began to feel the loneliness of the holidays once again. As Christmas came even closer, she decided to see her Threshold family. She admitted to herself that she missed them all, especially Rex. She called Benjamin to invite them over for Christmas Eve celebrations in the common area. She was worried about the publicity they would get but Benjamin reassured her that any publicity was good publicity and none of it mattered compared to being with Lily again.

On Christmas Eve, the Center was bustling with activity. The celebrations were to commence at six o'clock in the evening and consisted of non-alcoholic beverages and snacks provided by the Center. No food or beverages were allowed to be brought in from outside to prevent any unsanctioned consumption of alcohol or drugs. By three o'clock, Lily was more nervous than she was when she first met with Threshold what seemed like a lifetime ago. At that time, she had liquor to help her through it. She was nervous then about first impressions. Now she was nervous about letting her adopted family down. More than once, she considered calling to cancel, but each time Bernice and Corona were there to calm her down and reassure her.

By five-thirty, Lily was pacing around the common area. She went back to her room several times to check her appearance in the mirror. She touched up her lipstick three times. The center didn't generally allow make-up. They felt that it could be used as a mask to hide behind. They wanted people to feel confident in whom they were without any false enhancements. Since Christmas was a special occasion, patients were encouraged to look their best and allowed the frivolities of cosmetics. She wasn't certain about how her hair would be accepted since she had it cut very short since the last time anyone with the band saw her.

There was a knock at the door and she opened it to find a very happy Bernice. "Your friends are here," Bernice said.

Lily took several deep breaths, checked her appearance once more, touched up her lipstick again and went out to face the only people in the world that she cared about and would allow to care about her in return.

Chapter Eighteen

Lily smiled. "I hope this isn't breaking any rules."

"It's Christmas Eve! You can have as many guests as you want as long as they don't become too rowdy."

Patients and guests filled the common area. Bernice went to mingle with other patients who had guests and others who did not while Lily soaked in the warmth and affection of her adopted family. She did not want to admit how lonely she had been. She was also afraid that her friends would be a distraction from her recovery. She now realized how much she cared about them and that they genuinely cared about her. Everyone was trying to talk to her all at once. She finally had to raise her hands and wave for silence.

Lily started laughing. "Gee, I missed you guys. I really appreciate you coming to see me tonight. I know that everyone has other places they'd rather be than in here."

Benjamin stepped forward, characteristically taking control of the situation. "We wouldn't rather be anywhere else in the world than right here with you."

Others voiced their agreement and the hugging started. Everyone had brought presents and Kevin couldn't contain himself any longer. He burst forward and wrapped his arms around Lily's waist. He stepped back and thrust a gift bag at her.

"This is for you Miss Lily," Kevin said. "Where did all your pretty hair go?"

"Kevin!" exclaimed Cindy.

Lily laughed. She knelt down to be at eye level with Kevin and took his present.

"I gave my hair to someone who was sick and their medicine made their hair fall out. Some nice people will make a wig to make them look nice."

"Did medicine make Uncle Andy's hair fall out too?"

Cindy was very red in the face by now as everyone else laughed.

"No," laughed Lily. "Uncle Andy is just getting old and sometimes old people's hair just gets tired of growing."

"You're not getting your present!" shouted Andy with a laugh.

Lily stood up, still laughing and began to open Kevin's present.

"It was mine," said Kevin, "but I wanted you to have it. There's even a few already done that you can keep!"

Lily sat on the sofa so Kevin could sit next to her. Kevin reached in and helped her remove the wrapping paper out of the bag. Inside were a coloring book and a large box of crayons.

"Oh, Kevin, thank you!" Lily gave Kevin a hug and kiss. "I love it!"

"The book was mine," Kevin repeated, "but the crayons are new. There's even a sharpener on the bottom of the box if they get used up and you want them pointy again. Just remember to take some of the paper off first."

"Well, that's a very clever idea. Thank you again."

"Mommy said that you've been sick. When I'm sick, she makes me stay in my bed and I get bored, so I like to color to keep me busy. You don't look sick, Miss Lily. When are you coming home?"

Cindy interrupted, "That's enough questions now. Others want to give their gifts to Miss Lily too."

"That's all right," Lily reassured her. She looked at Kevin, "I was terribly sick but I'm much better now. I may come home in a few more weeks. I'll enjoy my new coloring book because I do get bored here sometimes."

"Mommy and Daddy brought you flowers!" Kevin jumped down and ran over to look at the Christmas tree.

Cindy went to keep a watch over her son while Peter stepped forward with a bouquet of flowers. It consisted of a beautifully arranged assortment of lilies, roses and delphiniums.

"Oh!" exclaimed Lily. "They're beautiful! I've never before seen all three combined before. Thank you!" She stood and hugged Peter.

Everyone took turns giving her various presents. Benjamin tried to outdo all the others by giving her a bottle of expensive perfume. Rex gave her a sketchbook and watercolors so she could continue her art. Mike saved his present for last. He stepped forward with a large white box tied with a red ribbon. Lily sat on the sofa again as she carefully untied the ribbon and lifted the lid. Inside the box, there was a beautiful violin.

"Oh, Mike," breathed Lily, "it's beautiful!"

She lifted it out and held it in her hands. She placed it under her chin and picked up the bow. It looked and felt like a natural extension of her.

"They were both made in Montreal."

"They are gorgeous!"

Lily laid them on her lap and wiped a tear. She looked up at Mike.

"I don't want to appear to be ungrateful. I love it. I really do, but isn't there something missing?"

Mike smiled. He handed her another small box. Lily opened it and smiled. Inside were the strings.

Mike explained, "This violin comes with no strings attached. We're giving it to you because we want you to have it. This is in no way to influence your decision on what you want to do after you get out of here."

Everyone laughed as Lily carefully moved aside the violin and stood to hug Mike.

"I don't think I've had so many hugs in one day," Lily said. "Thank you all for everything. I'm sorry that I haven't been able to get you guys anything. We made crafts before Christmas, but I think Kevin probably has the market on sticks and paper crafts. His are probably better."

Rex said, "The only gift we want from you is to get better and out of here."

Mike helped Lily attach and tune the strings to her new violin. Everyone else started to mingle with the patients who were beginning to gather because of the knowledge that Threshold was there. Lily scratched out a few notes and smiled.

The patients and guests sang Christmas carols and consumed the food and drinks provided by the Center. The party continued well into the evening. People started leaving after ten o'clock and they exchanged more hugs. Mike and Rex lingered after everyone else had left. They sat on the sofa quietly talking.

"Where's Cora and Pam tonight?" asked Lily.

"Cora's working until midnight but she sends her love," Mike said.

"Pam was invited to a new client's house for drinks," Rex told her.

"It's been quite a night," Lily said. "I'm tired." She smiled at her friends. "Thanks again."

"You're welcome," Mike said. "As we stated before, you're family and we just want you out of here. We'd love to have you come back to us, but even if you don't, you'll always be a part of us."

"I'm considering it," Lily told them. "The nurses are giving us looks. I think they want everyone to go home."

"Will you have us back to visit?" Rex asked her.

Lily blushed. She understood that he was asking if she would receive him the next time he stopped by.

"Yes. You guys may come back any time."

After her guests had all left, Lily relaxed in a hot bubble bath. After, she lay in bed exhausted. She avoided her emotions and hid from people most of her life. As a patient in rehab, she did more of the same. She suddenly had a new outlook on life. Her new family was no longer a distraction from her rehabilitation. They were now an inspiration. She decided that she would no longer turn them away. She would embrace them and love them freely. She now had an external force in her life that gave her reason and encouragement to leave rehab as soon as possible and start living her new life.

Lily was planning many changes and thinking about her new future as she fell peacefully asleep for the first time in years.

Chapter Nineteen

As the New Year progressed, so did Lily's recovery. She was now completely free of withdrawal symptoms and no longer required any medication. She took vitamin supplements and occasionally acetaminophen for her headaches. She was learning to control those headaches through physical therapy and exercise.

Lily now had to consider her discharge from the Center. She had only been in rehab for three months. Some patients take much longer but Lily was very young and very determined to be free of her demons. Based on how her counseling continued, her release was within the next several weeks. She had to make plans for her future in the real world. She was terrified. In the Center, there were no temptations and she had continuous support. She was afraid of failing and disappointing not only herself, but also her new family and the fans that had expressed concern for her.

One day, Lily was in her room working on a jigsaw puzzle when there was a knock at her door.

"Come in," Lily answered.

The door opened and Pam entered the room carrying an attaché case.

"Hi," Pam said. "I came as soon as I could."

Lily rose and crossed the room to give Pam a hug.

"Thanks for coming. I appreciate the promptness."

"I need to leave for Paris in a few days and I'm not sure how long I'll be gone. You sounded like you wanted to talk about something rather urgently, so I thought I'd come right away. I brought some ideas in regards to furnishings for your house."

"That's one of the things that I wanted to talk about. Please, have a seat."

Lily gestured toward the loveseat and they both sat down. Pam set her case on the coffee table in front of them.

"Before you open that case," Lily said, "I wanted to tell you of my decision."

"Which decision is that?"

"I want to give my house to Peter and Cindy."

"Why?"

"Peter has wanted to buy a house for his family for a long time. Without going into details, this house didn't cost me much so I wouldn't be losing a lot if I sold it to them for a very low price. I know you and Shawn worked hard on getting my house all fixed up and I'm sure it's more beautiful than before. I just can't go back there. There are too many memories and therefore too many temptations. I hope you understand that."

"I understand and appreciate that. What do you want to do?"

"I want to rent an apartment somewhere. I would like to be right in Chicago if possible. Can you use your connections to help me find a nice two bedroom place in a secure building?"

"That's no problem at all."

"I hate to ask."

"That's what family's for," Pam reassured her.

"I trust your judgment. Thank you."

"Anything to help out."

"Thanks. I need to discuss another important matter with you. It's a little difficult for me."

"Don't worry about it. Go ahead and ask."

"It was you that called Rex down to Bobbi-Jo's that night when you knew Threshold was looking for a singer. I never properly thanked you for turning my life around. If I hadn't have met any of you, I wouldn't have joined and I now wouldn't have the friends and family that I have now."

"Each road takes us closer to the path we're supposed to be on."

"All of you helped to save me from myself, even Tony in a weird sort of way. I'm a new person now because of everything that has happened. You are instrumental in my new life."

"All I did was tell Rex that you had a good voice and I thought they might want to interview you. It was you that did all the hard work."

"Rex was my first official contact with Threshold. He was there to help me out by driving me around and becoming my friend after Tony developed his problems. He was with me when I discovered my house vandalized and Jackson killed. He got me to the hospital and into this program. I feel like I owe my life to him."

"There's a little more to it that that," Pam told Lily. "Do you know who Rachael is?"

"She was Rex's younger sister who died several years ago."

"Rachael died of a drug overdose."

"I didn't know the details."

"Rachael was two years younger than Rex. The four of us did everything together. We were all supposed to be a team for life. Mike and Rachael were going to get married and Rex and I were going to get married. We all performed together at Bobbi-Jo's among other places. We loved to party. We were out of control many times but we had a handle on it. Rachael didn't. We didn't realize how out of control she was though. She was doing a lot of serious stuff and ended up addicted to cocaine. She would also do crack, ecstasy, heroin and anything else she could get her hands on.

"Rex found her unconscious on their bathroom floor. They rushed her to the hospital and pumped her stomach but the damage was already done. She stayed in a coma and died four days later.

"He never forgave himself. He always felt responsible for her death. He believed that if he had paid more attention to her he could have saved her.

"He sees Rachael in you. You're the little sister that he has to try to save. I think in saving you, he's somehow redeeming himself in his own eyes. That is why he has been so loyal to you. At first, I didn't want him to get so involved in case you didn't get through this. I'm glad now though for both of you. I'm not saying that you wouldn't have pulled yourself out of this on your own, but you said yourself that you feel that you owe your life to Rex. Maybe you do. I guess we will never really know. All I know is that I'm glad that you're all right and he is breathing a little easier too."

"I didn't realize all this, but it certainly makes sense now," Lily told Pam.

Lily remembered all the affection and that Rex showed her and his professed love for her. She understood now that it was Rex's mixed emotions and the love he truly felt for her was being confused with the brotherly love he lost with Rachael. It made her more aware of the situation.

"I wanted to ask you a question, but I'm not sure how to," Lily said.

"Just go ahead and ask."

"I need a Support Buddy after I get out of here. I need someone that I can trust and depend upon to help me through the tough spots when I stumble. Rex fits that description in my views but he's your husband and I don't want there to be any issues if I need help. I don't want any attention that he's supposed to be giving to you drawn away by my illness. The last thing I ever want to be is a burden to anyone. I don't know how much of my life Rex has told you."

"He's told me that you had a lot of horrors in your past but he wouldn't elaborate because he promised you he'd never reveal your secrets."

"I appreciate that you accept that. It scares me that I need to depend upon someone. I have never had anyone in my life that I could trust before, not even as a child. Tony tried to get close to me, but apparently, I read him correctly because I always suspected there was something about him I couldn't trust. I truly believe that Rex would never betray me or let me down."

"He wouldn't. He has taken responsibility for you in so many ways. You're everyone's little sister now and you have a whole family that you can trust. I can't think of a better person to be your Support Buddy. Besides, I travel a lot so he would be available for you without you feeling guilty about taking him away from me. Does this mean you're returning to Threshold?"

Lily smiled. "I've decided to return. Please don't tell anyone yet though. I want to be the one to break the news."

"I promise," Pam smiled. "I'm so happy things are better for you Lily. We were all so worried about you. The fact that Threshold's fans aren't losing you is also a huge relief to them. As for Rex, I'm sure he would be offended if you chose anyone else to support you. He has been doing a lot of self-healing through you. I think you can help each other."

"Thanks, Pam. When you see him, could you ask him to come and see me? Please don't mention this to him. I would like the idea to come from me. I don't want anyone else influencing his decision. I want him choosing for himself."

"I promise. Now, shall we discuss getting your lawyer to arrange the details of transferring ownership of your house over to Peter?"

Chapter Twenty

The day after Pam's visit, Lily was once again in her room. She had finished her puzzle after Pam had left and now she was coloring in the book that Kevin had given to her. She was relaxing after a particularly tough counseling session with Corona when there was a knock at her door.

"Come in," Lily called out.

The door opened and Rex stuck his head in.

"Hello."

Lily smiled. "Come in."

Rex entered the room with a single red rose. He closed the door and handed Lily the rose. She stood up to accept it and give him a hug. They held each other tight for several minutes. Finally, she stepped back and smelled the flower.

"It's beautiful. Thank you."

"I'm sorry that they didn't have any lilies, but I thought the rose was fitting."

Lily took it out of its packaging and put it in the vase with the flowers that others had given to her. She turned and smiled at him. He was admiring her coloring book. He looked up at her.

"I like your green and purple giraffe," Rex laughed.

"Thanks for coming so soon," Lily said and motioned to the loveseat. As he sat on the loveseat, she sat in the chair.

"Pam said that you wanted to see me right away," Rex told her.

"I do." Lily paused. "How are the shows going?"

"The fans miss you and hold up signs wishing you well. They accept Theresa though and give her incredible ovations. I admit that it's nice having her back but there's a void without you. I'm not pressuring you though," Rex smiled.

Lily returned his smile. "You're not pressuring me into anything. In fact, I have decided to come back, if you'll still have me."

Rex beamed and clapped his hands together. "That's wonderful news! I can hardly wait to tell everyone." Rex paused. "Or, did you want to tell them yourself?"

Lily shook her head. "You can have the fun of telling them."

"I'm so pleased. It hasn't been the same without you. I've missed you so much."

"I guess I owe you an apology."

"Whatever for?"

"You were there for me when I started detox and rehab. I turned you away. I shut you all out and I'm sorry for that."

"We understand that you did what you needed to do to protect yourself. You needed to get through this ordeal on your own and we respect that."

"Did Pam tell you why I wanted to see you?"

"No. She said that you would explain."

"When I get out of here, I won't be protected and sheltered anymore. I'll be dealing with new living accommodations that I haven't even secured yet. I need to set new routines and cope with loneliness and temptations. I'm learning new skills in here that I can take with me, but I don't know yet if I'll be able to put them into practice. I'm scared.

"I'm going to need someone to be my Support Buddy. I need to have someone that will be close by at all times that I can call upon when I find myself in trouble. I'll need someone to be by my side when I'm feeling weak, scared or tempted. I need someone that is able to drop everything and come running to me at a moment's notice. I need someone that I can literally put my life in their hands. That person that I would trust my life with is you. Would you be available or willing to be my Support Buddy?"

Rex stood up and crossed to where Lily was sitting. He took both of her hands into his and kneeled down to be at eye level with her.

"I would be honored and privileged to be there for you. I've promised to be there for you and as long as I draw breath I will support you in any way that I can."

"I'm concerned about the feelings that you have for me. I'm weak and vulnerable and I'm not sure if I'm capable of any kind of emotional involvement. I will need you to be tough with me. I may say some mean things to you. I need to know that this will work. Will we be able to get through this without hating each other afterwards?"

"I promise that whatever we have together will survive this. If you need me to be your Support Buddy, that's exactly what I'll be to get you through the tough times. If you need me to be a friend, that's what I'll be. If you need to be loved and comforted, I'll be there for that too. I promise to be whatever you need me to be."

"You'll need to meet with the councilors over the next several weeks so that they can train you and give you information you'll need to handle my situation. They will test you and screen you to make certain that you'll be good for me. These are really important steps."

"I understand and agree to all of this."

Lily paused, uncertain whether to bring up what was on her mind. Rex noticed but didn't want to be forceful. He let her decide to continue on her own.

"Pam told me all about Rachael," Lily finally said.

"You're not Rachael."

"No, I'm not. I need you to be clear on that. Whatever did or did not happen with your sister does not apply to me. I'm a different person in a different situation and I don't ever want to be confused with or compared to her."

"I promise you that also," Rex said as he released her hands and stood. "Where do I sign up?"

"I'm going to be getting out of here within the next few weeks. There's one more favor I want to ask of you."

"You name it."

Lily smiled.

Chapter Twenty-One

"Check your mirrors," Rex said.

Lily had been out of the Rehab Center for five weeks. She had rented an apartment in a very upscale building in an elegant neighborhood in Chicago based on Pam's advice. She paid Pam to furnish her apartment and she moved in on the very day that she was released. She was very happy in her new home. Spring weather arrived as the month of March began. Rex had been teaching her to drive for the past two weeks. They were in a little used area of a shopping mall parking lot.

"Signal and check over your shoulder before you pull out," Rex continued. "Make sure you're in first gear this time and let the clutch out slowly while easing down on the gas."

Lily slowly eased the car in motion. Lily never had an opportunity to drive before and was learning in Rex's sports car. She was terrified that she was going to damage it but Rex insisted that he teach her in his car.

"Why couldn't we borrow someone's automatic?" Lily winced.

"You have more advantages and opportunities open up for you if you know how to drive a manual transmission. Once you master this, you can drive an automatic very easily."

After another hour of practicing, Rex drove Lily home. Their friendship remained strictly platonic by silent agreement. Lily was adjusting well and as yet had no problems with any temptations. Rex pulled up to the front door of Lily's building and the concierge came out to assist Lily.

"Do you want to come in for awhile?" Lily asked Rex. "I could make us some supper."

"No, thanks. Maybe another time. I promised Pam I'd help her with some things."

"Alright. Another time then. Thanks again for the lesson." She leaned over and kissed him on the cheek. "I had fun."

"You should be ready to go for your driver's test soon. You're doing great."

"Thanks. What time is rehearsal tomorrow?"

"We're meeting at ten o'clock in the morning and having a group luncheon. Do you want me to pick you up?"

"No, thanks. I'll walk. Benjamin picked up my instruments yesterday and took them over to the sound stage."

"Are you nervous about coming back?"

"Are you kidding? I'm terrified."

"You've been with us for over a year."

"Yes, but I've been locked away for months. Also, I've never performed sober before."

"You'll do fine. Everyone's excited to have you back."

"Is Theresa going to be there?"

"I'm not sure what Benjamin has worked out with her."

"Can you ask her to be?"

"I can call her and see if she's planning to come. Why?"

"I really want Theresa to finish the tour."

"What? I thought you were coming back to us."

"I am. I just might freak out or something and want to have Theresa standing by to cover for me. Besides, I have an idea I'd like to throw at everyone."

The concierge cleared his throat indicating that he was still waiting to show Lily into her building. She smiled at Rex and winked.

"I guess we'll discuss this tomorrow," Lily told Rex.

Rex laughed as Lily got out of the car. She blew him a kiss and went into her building. Rex watched as she disappeared then smiled at the concierge and drove off towards home.

The next day, everyone arrived at the sound stage for rehearsals. Lily looked tired but excited to be there. She talked to everyone and hugged them as they went about their own business getting things ready to rehearse. Rex arrived a little late with Theresa in tow.

"It looks like everyone's here," Benjamin announced. "We'd all like to welcome Lily back."

Cheers and whistles sounded around the room.

"As you can see, Lily has personally requested Theresa to finish the tour. Are you or are you not returning to us Lily?"

"I'm returning. I was just thinking that, if Theresa is willing she could stay on for a while. The fans are used to her again. After all, she was the original female vocalist. Your original fans love having her back. She's here now and I'm sort of the one stuck in the middle that's connecting her here. It might be a nice treat for the fans to have us both. I'm willing to take a cut in pay to accommodate her."

"It's not the money," Benjamin said. "I'm willing to pay whatever it takes to give Threshold to the fans in any capacity. This is a band decision. I'll go along with whatever you decide amongst yourselves."

"I can't do this forever," Theresa said. "I left because I didn't want to do this anymore. I'm too old to tour and my vocal chords can't handle the abuse anymore. I admit that I've been having a lot of fun. I just feel that my time has passed and Lily is now the one to carry the torch."

"I think we can both carry it, at least for a few shows. I've added violin to the material and I'm excited about performing it live. I can't sing and play violin at the same time. If you're willing and everyone else approves, we could share the work. We can take turns singing lead and that will put less strain on your voice than doing it all. We can back each other up as well as give Mike a cool sound behind him with both of our vocals."

"I love the idea," Benjamin said, "but it will have to be up to Theresa. It would be the best of all worlds, but I'm a little biased. I love both you girls.

Theresa sighed. "I've made myself available to finish the North American part of this tour. It sounds like fun and I think we could make it work. I refuse to go to Europe with you guys though. That would be too much for me to handle."

Everyone voiced their agreements and excitement. They continued to discuss the possibilities and changes to the arrangements that would accommodate both female vocalists.

When they began to rehearse, things fell into place immediately. Lily had made herself familiar with the new material before coming and her self-taught violin talents added a lot more energy and dynamics to the old material as well. They worked everyday getting their parts worked out and by the end of April, they were ready to hit the road.

Threshold's first concert date was in Vancouver, British Columbia, Canada. It was a complete sell-out. Theresa was accepted by the audience once again as Lily's absence was now common knowledge and the fans reluctantly accepted her apparent departure.

Lily watched the show from backstage as Theresa worked the crowd and gave a terrific performance with the guys. She sang an incredible duet with Mike, and then they turned it up with an incredibly upbeat rocking tune. The crowd was wild with delight and Theresa quieted them by waving her hands.

"It's been incredible being able to rejoin Threshold," Theresa said, "and I'm really excited about this North American tour. It's great to be back! I've accepted the invitation to do this tour and I'm thrilled about it."

The fans screamed and whistled. When they quieted, Theresa continued.

"I thank everyone for their continued support, both fans and the band. I've missed performing for you Threshold fans. You're the best!"

Again, the fans cheered.

"I have one more announcement. I'm not doing this alone, people! I'm sharing the spotlight this time. Threshold fans, welcome back Miss Lily Rose!"

The whole auditorium exploded in frenzy. Fans screamed, danced and threw things. The thousands of fans cheered and whistled while Lily ran onto the stage with tears in her eyes. The band gathered around her, including Andy who stepped down from his drum platform. They all hugged and kissed her and Theresa handed her the microphone. Lily stood in front of thousands of adoring fans and waited until they settled down. The uproar continued, so Lily raised her hand and finally they fell silent.

"Thank you all," began Lily. "There's a lot I want to say. Please bear with me.

"First of all, I want to thank all the fans. Even though I can't possibly respond to all the communiqué and gifts that I have received while I was in the hospital, I appreciate every one. I read every note, card and email that I received and I've kept every gift and picture as well. Knowing how much you all care about me made my recovery so much more important."

Cheers again erupted from the crowd.

"Next, I need to thank everyone involved with Threshold and Beady Eye Productions. Not only did these guys on stage support me through this battle, so did all the technical crew members, office staff, management and their families that all made me feel a part of this much larger Threshold family."

More cheers erupted from the audience.

"I especially want to thank Theresa MacKenzie. She stepped up to the plate and covered for me. She continues to be there for me as we share the stage together. All I can say is, 'You rock, Girl!'"

The crowd once again went wild with disbelief that both ladies would be performing. Lily and Theresa hugged each other. The crowd became quiet when they saw that Lily had more to say.

"There's just one more thing that I need to say."

There was complete silence from the crowd.

"Ladies and Gentlemen, my name is Lily Rose Delphinium. I am an alcoholic and a drug addict and I've been sober for six months. Each day you live is a day closer to your death. It's up to you to choose how you want to live. If you or someone that you love has a problem, get help right away. Don't delay. Live life to the fullest and start today."

Chapter Twenty-Two

With the success of the Vancouver show, word traveled fast through the tabloids and entertainment news about the female duo that was now fronting Threshold. The band traveled in a convoy of touring buses and transport trucks. The band members were on one bus with a hired driver while the technical crew was on the second bus with various team members taking turns at the wheel. The two trucks had hired drivers. The first was a large transport truck and carried the staging, lighting and sound gear. The second smaller truck carried all of the band instruments.

After they left Vancouver, they went south back into the United States and headed for Seattle, Washington. From there they went to San Francisco, California; Las Vegas, Nevada; Boise, Idaho and finally in the month of April they played at Salt Lake City, Utah.

During travel times, everyone slept on the buses. When they arrived in the city they were playing at, they stayed in hotel rooms that had been booked well in advance for them and relaxed. While Mike and Rex did interviews and autograph sessions, everyone else either stayed in their rooms or went sightseeing. A few partied at the local bars but for Lily, it was a quiet stay in her room. She was rarely alone during their visits except when she slept. Rex constantly monitored her well-being and stress levels and a couple of the girls on the crew and Theresa often had girl-talk.

Lily offered to share a room with Theresa to save costs, but Andy, on behalf of Beady Eye, approved the spending so each singer could have privacy and complete rest. Mike and Rex always shared a room as did Andy and Peter. The rest of the crew and the drivers also doubled up when staying in hotels.

By the middle of May, they had performed in Phoenix, Arizona; Albuquerque, New Mexico; and Denver, Colorado. They arrived in Houston, Texas two days before their show and everyone was extremely tired. They arrived quite late and were anxious for showers and a long sleep in a real bed.

Upon arriving at the hotel, everyone scattered to their assigned rooms. Lily entered hers and was impressed that Andy booked her a luxurious suite. She dropped her bags and went to examine her surroundings. She appreciated the gesture and the fact that they had a few days to stay there. She hoped that Theresa was getting the same royal treatment.

Lily was very tired. She found the traveling and the performing exhausting. Everyone else was also tired but she had the added daily battle of fighting her addictions. As though the demons in her life were taunting her, she opened the mini fridge and found it stocked with individual alcoholic beverages. She slammed the door shut. She couldn't believe her eyes. She took a few deep breaths then reopened the fridge. She didn't imagine it. There, within easy grasp were the bottles. She kneeled down and continued to stare at them. Finally, she reached out and ran her fingers across the tops of them. She stopped at a tiny bottle of rum, which was her favorite.

Lily pulled her hand away quickly as if the bottle burned her. She stood up and closed the door again. She began to pace around the room, rubbing her arms. She began to tremble, feeling cold but feverish. She was experiencing withdrawal symptoms after being sober for several months. She tried to remember if her councilors told her that this could happen, but she couldn't.

The fridge seemed to be calling to her. Lily went back and sat on the floor, facing the fridge. After hesitating for several minutes, she opened the fridge again. She stared at the bottles for a few more minutes. Finally, she reached in and touched the bottle of rum. Her fingers seemed to wrap themselves around it against her will.

"What am I doing?" Lily asked herself.

Despite her effort to resist, the bottle ended up in Lily's hand and she continued to sit on the floor, the fridge door still open. She looked at the bottle and turned it repeatedly in her hands. She could feel her mouth begin to water as she remembered the taste of it and the feel of it coursing through her veins.

"I've been clean for seven months," Lily reminded herself. "But it's such a small bottle. Maybe if I just smell it."

Slowly, Lily turned the cap. It loosened too easily. Soon, the cap was off and she was deeply inhaling the aroma of the rum. It smelled good and her heart rate increased with the excitement and fear she was experiencing. The trembling stopped and she convinced herself that there was no harm in smelling it. The next step wasn't far behind.

"If I just stick my finger in and have a little taste, that will be alright,"

Her pinkie finger fit inside the neck of the bottle. The rum moistened it and she removed it and put it in her mouth. She closed her eyes in ecstasy. It tasted incredible.

"It's such a small bottle," Lily repeated to herself.

She raised the bottle to her lips and began to tip it into her mouth.

....

Rex was in the shower when his cellular phone began to ring. It was on top of the hotel dresser and it rang several times before Mike found it. He had fallen asleep while waiting for Rex to finish in the bathroom. Mike answered Rex's phone.

"Hello?"

There was unintelligible babble on the other end.

"Hello? Who is this?"

Mike couldn't understand any words but upon listening closely realized it was a woman crying.

"Pam? Is that you? This is Mike. Who is this? Please calm down. I can't understand you."

"…Lily…"

"Lily, where are you? What's wrong?"

"…Rex…"

"Rex is in the shower. Lily, what's wrong?"

Lily was in hysterics and Mike could only understand a few words that she was saying.

"…help…"

"Are you in your hotel room?"

"…yes…"

"We'll be right there. Don't go anywhere!"

Lily disconnected the line so Mike pocketed Rex's phone. He pounded on the bathroom door with his fist.

"Rex!" Mike shouted.

He continued to pound and call out until Rex opened the door, dripping wet with a towel held in front of him.

"What's wrong?" Rex asked.

"I'm not sure but I think Lily's in trouble. She's in her room and needs help. I'm on my way."

"I'll be right behind you."

Mike ran out of the room and dashed for the stairs. He took them two at a time and went up two levels to the floor on which Lily's suite was located. Rex turned off the water, managed to get his jeans on over his wet body, and fastened them as he left the room. His hair was still dripping and he was barefoot and bare-chested. He also ran up the stairs to Lily's suite.

When Rex arrived, Mike was still pounding on Lily's door. Finally, she opened it fell into Mike's arms. She was trembling and her eyes were red and swollen. She continued to sob uncontrollably.

"Lily," Rex asked, "are you hurt?"

Lily shook her head. Mike led her over to the sofa and helped her to sit. She refused to let go of him so he continued to hold her. Once Rex made certain that she wasn't injured or in danger, he looked around the room for any clues as to what had happened. He found several empty liquor bottles on the counter, in the sink and on the floor. The strong smell of alcohol suddenly hit him and he figured out what was wrong. Lily had a breakdown and got drunk.

Rex went over to Lily and Mike and kneeled on the floor in front of them. He took her hand and held it to his lips.

"It's alright. Things happen. We'll take care of you."

Lily sobbed and hiccupped as she tried to talk.

"It's alright," Rex continued. "Just take deep breaths. I'll do it with you."

Rex assisted Lily with the breathing techniques they learned at the Rehab Center to calm her down. After several minutes, she stopped hyperventilating and began to calm down.

Chapter Twenty-Three

"I didn't know what to do."

"It's alright," Rex repeated. "Just tell us what happened."

"I opened the fridge and there they were." Lily gestured toward the kitchenette.

"The fridge was stocked with booze?" Mike asked.

Lily nodded.

"When Andy booked each hotel, he made certain that all the rooms were alcohol-free. Obviously, this was a terrible oversight. I'll let Andy know and he can take it up with the management."

"I know," Rex began, "this is very hard."

"You have no idea how hard it is," Lily sobbed.

"No, we don't," admitted Mike.

"I hurt all the time. I can't even take my own pain meds."

Rex had control over her medication and kept them with him at all times. He dispensed them to her when she needed something for her headaches.

"I'm scared all the time," Lily continued. "Every morning when I wake up, I need a drink. Every night when I go to bed, I need a joint. All day, every day, I think about drinking. I need a drink all the time. I'm so scared of failing. I'm scared of letting myself down after all the effort and time I've put into my sobriety. I don't want to let the band down and I certainly don't want to let my fans down. Some of the letters I've received are from people who admitted to having a problem with addiction and they say that I'm an inspiration to them. I don't want to be put up on a pedestal. It's too far to fall."

"You only have to be accountable to yourself," Rex said.

"Maybe," said Lily, "but it was you guys and the fans that gave me the strength to do what I did tonight."

Rex and Mike looked at each other in confusion.

"What you did tonight?" Mike asked.

"I poured all that booze down the drain!"

A huge smile broke out on Rex's face.

"You didn't drink any of it?"

"No," Lily started crying again. "I came so close though. I had the bottle to my lips and I was going to drink it. I just wanted to feel that buzz again. I'm tired of feeling this way. I'm not happy anymore and I wanted to be drunk again so I could just feel happy again."

Rex pulled her into his arms away from Mike. He gave her a huge hug and continued to hold her tight, running his hands through her hair.

"Oh, Dora, I'm so proud of you! That was the bravest and hardest thing you could have done!"

"Dora?" asked Mike.

"I'm so proud of you!" Rex repeated, ignoring Mike. "You do remember being told that giving up your addiction is very much like grieving. You'll have good days and bad and you need to work through the grieving process of losing a part of you. It was a destructive part of you, but it was a part of you none the less."

Lily lay in Rex's arms and soon stopped crying. Seeing the tenderness between them, Mike felt uncomfortable and out of place. He decided to leave them alone.

"Are you going to be alright?" Mike asked her.

"Yes, thank you for coming so fast."

"That's what friends are for. I think I'll leave you in Rex's capable…" he paused as he looked at their embrace, "…hands. Call anytime at all that you need me. I'm here for you too."

"Thank you, Mike."

Lily gently broke out of Rex's hold and gave Mike a big hug. He held her for a moment and then left, making sure the door closed behind him.

After Mike left, Lily continued to lie in Rex's arms. She was exhausted and neither she nor Rex seemed to have anything left to say. She would cry for a while then doze off. When she awakened, she would begin to cry again. Rex felt helpless to do anything for her, so he continued to hold her and stroked her hair. All he could do was let her know that she was safe and loved.

Eventually, Rex also fell asleep. He awoke with a start and realized that Lily was no longer beside him on the couch.

"Lily?"

Rex sat up and looked around. Lily had turned off all the lights except for the light over the sink. In the dim light, he saw her sitting on the floor in the kitchenette holding a couple of the empty bottles. He walked over to her and crouched down beside her.

"What are you doing?" Rex asked.

Lily shrugged. "I don't know."

Rex stood up and offered Lily his hands.

"Come on. Get up."

Lily dropped the bottles onto the floor and took his hands, allowing him to help her stand. She leaned into his arms and nuzzled his neck.

"You've had a rough night," Rex said softly. "Why don't you go to bed and try to get some sleep."

"I don't want to be alone."

"You won't be. I'll stay here with you."

Lily held Rex tightly and lowered her head. This time Rex found Lily's neck.

"I will never leave you," Rex whispered into her ear.

They moved together and found each other's lips. As they kissed, her hands moved across his bare muscular chest and arms.

"Come to bed with me."

After they made love, Lily lay in Rex's arms, her head resting on his chest. He ran his fingers through her hair.

"You have a very strong heart," Lily said, listening to his chest.

"I like to stay in shape."

"Yes, I can see that," Lily said as she felt his biceps.

"It's nice to see you feeling better."

"That was much better than a joint."

They lay quietly for several minutes, enjoying the feel of each other's bodies next to each other.

"I guess if anyone asks," Lily said, "we talked all night."

"I could have slept on the couch."

"Anyone who looks at you can tell that you haven't slept."

"I'd like to sleep, here next to you."

"It's going to be strange to everyone who sees you in the morning returning to your room from mine half undressed. I'm fine now. It'd probably be best if you left now while no one's around."

"I don't want to leave yet."

They lay quietly for several minutes.

"Can I make a confession?" Lily asked.

"Always."

"I don't want to weird you out."

"Now, I'm scared."

"Tonight was the first time that I willingly gave myself to someone while I was sober."

"You honor me. I mean that."

"Now, can I ask something?"

"Anything."

"Does it bother you to be with me now that you know what I was and the things that I did?"

Rex turned Lily so he could look at her. He continued to stroke her hair tenderly and kissed her.

"I'm in love with you. Your past means nothing to me. This beautiful woman in my arms that I've gotten to know and love is the woman that I want to be with."

"My past will always be a part of who I am."

"I accept your past along with your present and future."

"It's your past, present and future, Rex, that you need to concern yourself with, not mine. This can cause great pain to some very innocent people."

Rex lay back down and Lily once again settled in his arms. They remained quiet again.

"What about your future?" Rex asked, breaking the silence. "Don't you want to get married and have a baby someday?"

"I never thought about it. My future always consisted of when and where I'd get my next fix."

"Now that you're clean?"

"I still don't have any plans. I'm just going to take things as they come. That's all I can do. Everything else is too lofty for me."

"Why?"

"I'm already living on borrowed time, Rex. I really don't know how much time I have left."

"None of us do."

"At this second in time, I'm completely content and satisfied but that has everything to do with you. I need to learn to continue on my own and depend only on myself. You can't be with me every second of every day. You have other obligations."

"You've come a long way in such a short time. You could go back to school. Having a family is one of the most natural things in life. You're young and healthy. You have your whole life ahead of you. You can do anything you decide to do."

"You don't understand. My body has been abused in ways most people couldn't even imagine. I've been sexually abused and addicted to drugs and booze since I was a kid. It's extremely doubtful that I could even get pregnant. Even if I could, I wouldn't want to bring an innocent life into this world only to have it grow up without a mother. I've been beaten, stabbed and have had my skull smashed in. I still have bone fragments embedded in my brain. I could fall, bang my head or even sneeze and if those fragments shift, I could be paralyzed or even dead in seconds.

"All of this has been a big part of what I had to accept as a part of my sobriety. If you plan to be my friend, you'll have to understand and accept all of this, too."

"Every day that I spend with you is a gift."

Rex kissed Lily passionately. As they began to make love again, Rex whispered in her ear.

"A hundred years or a hundred hours, I want to spend it all with you."

Chapter Twenty-Four

Despite the shaky beginning in Houston, the show went extremely well. Lily was the most relaxed and energetic she had been the entire tour and the rest of the band and the fans found her energy contagious. The rest of the band knew about Lily's near disaster although they managed to keep it from the public. Everyone who worked with Lily was sensitive to her situation and voluntarily agreed to remain chemical free in her presence for the remainder of the tour.

Very few travel mates found it suspicious over the next few weeks when Lily needed to have quiet alone time with her Support Buddy. They realized that she kept her emotions bottled up inside her and it was destroying her. Her temptation had become too strong and wasn't turning to Rex, as she needed to. They were happy to see her finally getting the support that she had avoided accepting. Mike had his own suspicions, but his loyalties were divided amongst his support of Lily as their lead singer, his best friend who was like a brother and his sister. He kept quiet but remained cool to them.

Threshold traveled to Des Moines, Iowa and then to Detroit, Michigan. After the show in Detroit, they had an entire week to travel the short distance to their next show in Canada. They had no problems at Customs and decided to take their time and enjoy the distance to Toronto. Everyone enjoyed the warm June weather in Southern Ontario.

They arrived in Toronto three days before their scheduled concert. They visited the venue at which they were going to perform and confirmed all the arrangements as well as checked over the requirements for their show. Mike and Rex left to do some interviews and appearances. The crew stayed at the venue and that left Peter, Andy, Lily and Theresa with time to spend however they liked.

"What a great city!" exclaimed Peter as they began to walk. "There's so much to see and do. Where do we begin?"

"I don't know about you guys," Theresa began, "but I would love to check out the baseball stadium here. I hear it's a great place to see a game. Do you guys want to go?"

Peter was a life-long Cubs fan so he was interested in checking out the Toronto Blue Jays.

"They aren't my Cubs and they aren't in the National League, but it sounds like a lot of fun. I'm in. How about you two?"

"I'm not a big baseball fan," answered Andy. "There's just not enough action. Sorry, but I find baseball boring."

"Unlike cars going around in circles for hours," quipped Theresa in reference to Andy's following of the NASCAR Cup series.

"Hey, it's not just cars going in circles. You have to understand horse power, gear ratios, the physics of air down force, degrees of tire cambers, weather effects on the track…"

"Yeah, yeah," interrupted Theresa, "but they're still going in circles."

"Not if they're on a road course," laughed Andy.

"I give up!" Theresa exclaimed playfully. "How about you, Lily? Do you want to come to the ball game with Peter and me?"

"No, thank you," answered Lily. "I've had a headache all day. I'd like to relax somewhere quiet. I may just go back to the hotel."

"Maybe we could get some dinner," suggested Andy.

"That sounds good. I am feeling hungry."

"So am I," Theresa said. She turned to Peter. "Let's go get a couple of hotdogs at the game."

Peter and Theresa left for the game and Andy and Lily began to walk. There were a lot of people as they turned onto Yonge Street. They window shopped at various stores and checked out the wares of roadside vendors. They saw a large music store and laughed at themselves in a Threshold concert promotional poster in the window. They were recognized several times and obliged the attention with autographs and photos. They decided on a little restaurant on a side road and settled into a corner booth. The waitress left them with menus as they refused drinks.

"Are you looking forward to getting back to Chicago?" Andy asked.

"Yes, I am. This is the first time in my life that I've ever done this sort of thing. I can't believe how tiring it is. I could sleep for a week."

"I wish I could. When we get home, I have to go straight to work at Beady Eye and catch up on the backlog of accounting work that's been piling up since we left. I'm getting too old to do this anymore."

"You're not that old," Lily flattered him.

"I'm forty-four years old, Lily. You and Peter are babies compared to me. My children are around your age."

The waitress came back and took their orders. After she left, they continued their conversation.

"You and I don't really have many opportunities to talk," Andy complained.

"I know. We've been working together for quite awhile now and we call ourselves a family. I guess it's true with any family though. There's always going to be some people that are closer than others."

"Rex has really come through for you."

"Yes, he has," Lily agreed. "I would never have imagined anyone sacrificing so much of themselves to help me through this."

"It's something any of us would have done."

"Oh, I realize that. I didn't mean any disrespect to anyone else."

"That's not how I meant it. We're all here for you is what I meant to say."

After their food arrived, they ate in silence for awhile.

"I'm sorry to say that the tabloids are really having a field day with you," Andy informed Lily.

"I'm not surprised. These people come up with the craziest things. I'm sure women having three-headed alien babies have more truth to it than what they can dig up about me." Lily laughed, trying to hide her concern and discomfort. "I don't read those things and I really don't want to know what's in them."

"You'd probably be better off not knowing."

"Maybe you should tell me, just so I know what I'm dealing with should anything come up."

"Just crazy things like you were a drug-addict child prostitute."

Lily immediately started choking on her food. As she gasped for air, Andy ran around to help her and drew the attention of patrons and staff alike. She waved everyone off and reached for her water. After a few frightening moments, she cleared her throat.

"I'm so sorry," Andy said. "That was very insensitive of me. I just didn't think."

"That's alright," Lily replied, wiping her eyes and drinking her water.

After proving that she was fine, everyone settled back down. The waiter lingered a few minutes longer to ensure that his customer was truly alright. Lily reassured him and he finally left.

"I really am sorry," Andy repeated.

"That's really ok. I asked you to tell me."

"You probably don't want to hear the other stuff then."

"It can't possibly be worse than that," Lily said, adding a forced laugh.

"I'll tell you if you want to hear it."

"You're just dying to tell me," Lily chided him. "I can see the twinkle in your eyes."

"It's a continuation of your 'affair' with Mike."

"Oh, that. Poor Cora."

"Funny enough, she really doesn't mind. Not very many people have that kind of trust in their relationship."

"So, how hot and heavy are we now?"

"Still at it about the same. Must be great sex. It's been widely observed that you have the glow of a very happy and sexually satisfied woman."

Lily could feel her face turn red with embarrassment.

"I think I'd rather not hear the rest, please"

Andy laughed. "Now I embarrassed you completely. At least you didn't choke this time. Actually, you do look much healthier and happier since you became sober. I can see why people would think that, especially with your act with Mike." Andy paused. "Are you planning on staying with Threshold for awhile?"

"I'm not really sure what I want to do. I've been given a new lease on life. As fun and as exciting this has been I don't know how long I want to do it. What about you?"

"I've been talking to Mike and Rex and told them that I've decided that this is my last tour. If they want an occasional drummer for something, I'll do it, but my hands are full at Beady Eye. My kids are all grown up with lives of their own and I don't get to see them very much. My son is talking about getting married and if I'm going to be a grandfather someday, I want to be available to be one."

"I haven't said anything to anyone," Lily said, "but I'd like to do something meaningful. Not that entertaining thousands of fans isn't meaningful. It's actually more rewarding than I could have imagined. I finished high school through computer correspondence but I never went to college. I'd like to help people who suffer with addictions. The councilors at the Rehab Center were wonderful and I'd like to make a difference somehow. Who better to trust and open up to than another alcoholic and addict?"

"I think that you would be wonderful doing that."

They finished their dessert and walked back to the hotel. They went to their separate rooms and Lily went to bed. She still had a headache and wanted to rest. After awhile, a knock at her door awakened her.

"Who's there?" Lily called out.

"It's Rex. Can I come in?"

Lily closed her eyes and sighed. She turned on the bedside lamp and got out of bed. She put on her robe and went to the door. She released the safety chain, unlocked the deadbolt and opened the door.

"Hi," Lily greeted Rex.

Rex entered the room, noticing her unmade bed.

"I'm sorry. I woke you up. Are you all right?"

"I've got a headache and I'm really tired."

"Have you taken something for your headache?"

Lily gave him a look that showed annoyance.

"What I have access to, I took." Lily replied. "I just need some sleep."

"What did you do after you left the concert hall?"

"Andy and I had dinner. Afterwards, I came here and went to bed."

"I missed you today."

Rex moved and began to take Lily in his arms but she pulled away.

"Not tonight. I don't feel well."

"Okay. Do you need anything at all?"

"Sleep."

Rex smiled. "How about breakfast in bed?"

"We need to talk. I'm too tired tonight though. Are you free to come by here about nine o'clock tomorrow morning?"

Rex looked concerned. "Alright. I'll see you at nine."

Rex tried to kiss Lily but she turned her head. He ended up kissing her cheek.

"Sweet dreams." Rex said as he left.

Lily closed the door. Again, she turned the deadbolt and fastened the safety chain before she went back to bed. Her headache suddenly became much worse.

....

Promptly at nine o'clock the next morning, Rex knocked at Lily's hotel room. When she opened the door, she looked much healthier and more rested than the night before.

"Wow! You look better," Rex said. "Good morning."

"I had a great sleep. Even my headache's gone."

"That's great. I was worried about you. Did you have breakfast?"

"I had a muffin and a coffee. Please, sit. Let's talk."

Rex and Lily sat on the edge of the bed and faced each other. Lily took his hand.

"What's wrong?" asked Rex. "What do you want to talk about?"

"Us."

"What about us?"

"There can't be an 'us' anymore. The sex has to stop."

"I thought that we were good for each other."

"We're good with each other. That's different. Our situations in the real world haven't changed. I care about you but I'm still not strong enough for this. This whole tour has been an incredible fantasy. I still need to find my way alone and you have other obligations. I have to be honest with myself as well as you. I've been using you. You are a safe person to be with and I trust you. My whole life I've been avoiding life by losing myself in drugs. Lately, I've been losing myself in you. You are incredibly sweet and gentle."

"That's the way it's supposed to be."

"We have to end this before it destroys our friendship. We're returning home after this Toronto show. We can't be together anymore."

"This is very hard for me too," Rex confessed. "I love you. I also love Pam. I'm torn to pieces over my mixed emotions."

"There's a difference between true love and infatuation, Rex. True love will always be at home waiting for you to return. Don't ever throw away that kind of love. It happens so rarely in life."

Rex began to cry. "I don't know what to do."

"Yes, you do," Lily comforted him. She put her arms around him and he rested his head on her chest. "You go back home and be with Pam. I once told you that I could never love you. I care about you but I'm not willing to ruin your marriage. I'm also not willing to ruin our friendship. I still need you, but I'll understand if you need to walk away from me completely."

Rex lifted his head and looked at her.

"No. I promised you that I would be anything you needed me to be. I've fulfilled that promise on many levels and I will continue to support you. I'm not willing to lose our friendship either. You mean too much for me and I love you enough to respect your wishes."

"So, are we going to be okay?"

Rex smiled. "We're going to be okay."

Chapter Twenty-Five

It was very early in the morning when Rex arrived home. He unlocked the door quietly, not wanting to awaken Pam. He was excited to be home, but was nervous about seeing his wife again. His experience with Lily seemed to heighten his awareness of his feelings for Pam and he was anxious to begin anew at rekindling their relationship. He stepped into the kitchen to find Pam already up and having coffee at the table, reading the newspaper.

"You're up!"

"Of course, I'm up. I'm driving back to New York today."

Pam put her coffee down. "Welcome home."

Rex set his suitcases down and rushed over to her.

"I've missed you so much."

Rex lifted Pam to her feet, picked her up, and swung her around.

"Put me down!"

Rex lowered her feet to the floor but did not let go of her. He squeezed her tight and began to kiss her neck and face.

"You smell so good. You look wonderful," Rex told her.

Pam pulled away from him.

"I'm really glad you got home before I had to leave. We need to talk."

Rex felt a sudden heaviness in his heart. The last time someone said those words to him, he was left broken hearted and depressed. A feeling of dissolution came over him. Pam gestured to the chair across from where she had been sitting. When they both sat, Pam began to speak.

"As you know, I spend a lot of time now in New York on business."

"Yes," Rex answered hesitantly.

"I've decided to buy an apartment there."

"Can we afford that?"

"I can afford it. I have never used any of your money for my business."

"It's our money. What's mine has always been yours."

"Not anymore. I have always been completely self-sufficient with Mitchell-Landers. It was the only way I could succeed. My business is mine, my car is mine and my apartment will be mine. I've leased an office space in New York and have hired three full-time designers and an office manager to handle things while I travel."

"This is really good news. I knew you would be a success at this. I'm proud of you. I have to confess that with me so busy with the band, I didn't really have time to keep up with you and your news."

"We haven't exactly been in the same place at the same time lately."

"I know and I'm sorry," Rex apologized. "This tour will be ending soon and I promise that I'll spend more time with you. We can get to know each other all over again. We can have new beginnings."

"I'm moving to New York."

"What?"

"I can't grow as much as I'd like to here. I'm relocating Mitchell-Landers Designs to New York City where I will live and work."

"I support you in every decision that you make, but I'm not ready to leave Chicago just yet. I still have a lot of obligations here…"

"You're not coming with me," Pam interrupted. "All I'm taking is my car and my personal belongings. You can have the house and everything in it."

Rex was speechless for a few minutes.

"You don't have to leave," Rex suggested. "You can split your time between Chicago and New York. You already said that you hired an office manager."

"I'm tired of doing that. The truth is that I'm having the time of my life. I've been meeting so many new people and traveling to places that I thought I would only dream about. It's time that I go out on my own. Our life here together has been good, but I've got a taste of excitement and freedom and I want to explore on my own what I can do with my life."

"Are you leaving me?" Rex asked with disbelief.

"Yes."

"But you're my wife!"

"…and you're my husband because that's what everyone expected us to be. We have always been friends and we will probably always be friends. Our relationship was based on the safety we had with each other and what everyone else wanted for us. We never questioned it. We were all we knew. After Rachael died, it fell upon us to carry through with the fantasies we had as kids; you and me; Mike and Rachael. We made a good team and we made a nice looking couple. Our marriage was arranged and we just went along for the ride. We loved each other like brother and sister. There was never any passion between us. Everything we did was comfortable and safe. There was no risk involved in anything we did.

"Well, now I've discovered a passionate side of me that I didn't know existed. I'm passionate about my business and I'm passionate about taking some personal risks as well. I love what my life has developed into and I have you to thank for all of it. You gave me support and helped me to build confidence in myself. I need to be free to follow my passions. You need to be free to follow yours."

"What do you mean?" Rex asked.

"I always felt that something was missing in our marriage. I thought it was children but I realized what was missing the day Lily fell into our lives. You had a lighter step, an easier smile and a brighter twinkle in your eye. At first, I thought that you had found in Lily the sister you lost in Rachael. I thought you were happier feeling needed by someone. I was too independent and you now had a cause to fight for. As time went on, I realized that you had found in Lily what you never found in me. Finally, I admitted to myself that you were in love with her."

"Pam, Lily isn't…"

"It's all right," Pam interrupted. "At first, I was scared and confused, hurt and disappointed. Then I saw it as new beginnings for both of us. We've reached our threshold. It's time for change. We both need to move on and accept new challenges. We need to close this chapter in our lives."

A tear rolled down Rex's cheek. He wiped it away.

"I don't want to lose you," Rex whispered.

"Don't make this any harder. It's what's best for both of us."

"What happens now?"

"My lawyer has already drawn up the divorce papers. All you have to do is sign them and we're both free to pursue our own dreams. As I've said, I've left everything for you and I will not come back for any property or finances. I just want a clean break."

Pam got up from the table and retrieved her briefcase from the office. She opened it and took out the divorce papers. She handed them to Rex and proceeded to get ready to leave for New York. She opened the door and picked up her bags. As she began to leave, she turned back to Rex. He was still sitting at the table with the papers in his hand, looking like a truck just drove over his heart.

"I'll collect the rest of my things in a few weeks. Take care of yourself. Take care of her."

The door closed behind Pam and Rex continued to sit in a state of shock. He stared at the closed door through which he forever lost his wife and best friend.

Chapter Twenty-Six

Threshold had three days at home in Chicago before their performance for their hometown fans. The venue had already been set up and the crew and performers were arriving in the afternoon of the show for sound checks. Once everyone else had arrived, it was obvious that Lily was missing.

"She had something to do," Rex informed the others. "She promised to get here as soon as possible and offered her apologies. We'll get started and she can do her checks when she arrives."

Band and crew worked together flawlessly for two hours. Once everything checked out, they decided to practice some new material that Mike and Rex had been working on. After another hour, Lily arrived flustered and winded.

"I'm so sorry I'm late," Lily apologized. "One of the problems with living in a city is that there are so many people to contend with. I'm ready for my checks."

Lily completed her sound checks and they continued to rehearse and try out new songs. They decided to wrap up for supper and relax before their concert. Rex approached Lily but she pretended not to see him. She started whistling and doing unnecessary tidying around her area. He folded his arms across his chest and tapped his foot. She attempted to continue to ignore him and ended up laughing instead.

"All right," Rex demanded. "Let's see it."

"See what?" Lily asked innocently.

"I want to see if it's possible for the most beautiful woman in the city to have a bad photograph."

Lily laughed. "It's quite awful. Trust me."

Mike, who had been watching their banter, decided that it was time for him to join in.

"What's going on here?" Mike demanded in a false stern voice. "No fighting in the venue. It's bad for publicity."

Lily and Rex began to laugh.

"Lily just got her Driver's License," Rex informed Mike.

"Look out everyone!" Mike shouted. "Lily's officially on the road!"

Her friends and colleagues screamed and joked with her. They also sincerely congratulated her. Soon everyone began to leave.

"I'm very proud of you," Rex told Lily. "This is just one more accomplishment in a series of so many."

"I'm proud of myself," Lily admitted. "The things that I've done have surprised me. I never gave myself a chance because I wasn't sober long enough to even make any kind of plans or be responsible enough to even get behind the wheel of a car."

"I think it was very responsible of you to not drive. A lot of people don't recognize that they are unable to drive while intoxicated."

"I'm not sure about that. I was never in situations where I had an opportunity to drive. Either way, I've never earned that privilege so I never missed it. Now that I'm sober, so many more possibilities have opened up to me that I never dreamed possible before."

"This calls for a celebration. Please, let me take you to dinner tonight. I'm buying."

"Is Pam out of town again?"

"She's in New York."

"In that case, you've got yourself a date."

"You're driving though."

They were walking through the parking lot when Rex suddenly stopped.

"I'm losing my mind!" Rex exclaimed. "I didn't drive here today. Mike drove me!"

Lily began to laugh hysterically. Rex looked at the keys in his hands.

"I guess we'll have to take your car then!" Rex said as he threw the keys toward Lily. She caught them and looked at him, confused.

"What are you talking about?" Lily asked.

Rex put his hand on a shiny new black sports car.

"This baby is yours," Rex explained.

"You're not serious!"

"I knew you'd get your license so I bought you this car. It's been sitting here for a couple of days, waiting patiently for its new owner to take it home."

"It's beautiful!" Lily ran her hand over the smooth exterior. "I can't accept this."

"Of course you can."

Rex took Lily by the hand and guided her to the driver's door.

"Get in," Rex told her. "I've been dying to see you in it."

Lily nervously unlocked the door and opened it. She breathed in the new car smell and felt the softness of the leather interior. She was giddy as she slid into the seat and placed her hands on the steering wheel. Rex took out his i-phone and took some pictures of her in her new car.

"I don't know what to say."

"Say, 'Thank you.'"

"I don't know."

"I'm not trying to buy your affections. I just wanted to do this for you."

"But the cost!"

"I can afford it."

"What about Pam?"

"She's already got a car."

"I mean, does she know about this? She's bound to care about the money."

"Pam and I have an agreement. Trust me. She won't care. May I get in?"

"Yes, of course."

Rex got into the passenger seat. After the doors closed, Lily began to cry.

"Hey, what are the tears for?" Rex asked.

"No one has ever done anything like this for me before. I feel like I should owe you something in return."

"Absolutely not. You have earned this. This is something that I wanted to do for you. The only thing you have to do in return is to continue to be my friend and to drive safely. All you have to do to make it yours is go with me tomorrow to the Ministry of Transportation and switch over the ownership from me to you. You'll also have to get your own insurance. Right now, it's under mine. Come here."

Lily leaned over and allowed Rex to wrap his arms around her. She put her head on his chest and immediately they both felt the attraction that they had for one another. She lifted her head and brushed his lips with her. As tempted as he was, he was not going to make her feel as though she owed him anything. After a quick kiss, he pulled away.

"As much as I love holding you," Rex whispered, "I'm very hungry. Let's get to that restaurant and celebrate with the best ginger ale they have in stock."

Laughing, Lily started the car. She appreciated the gentle rumble of its powerful engine. Easing the car into gear, she drove out of the parking lot into rush hour traffic.

Chapter Twenty-Seven

During the summer break, the members and crew of Threshold had four weeks to catch up on their personal and professional 'to do' lists. Each person's agenda differed greatly from each other. Some used the time to relax with family and others were busy working at other projects.

Cora planned her three-week vacation to correspond with Threshold's break and she and Mike used the time to go to Mexico for a well-deserved vacation together. Peter worked a few local gigs to supplement his income but mainly enjoyed being at home with Cindy and Kevin. They loved living in Lily's old house and Kevin was still excited about the secret room that they turned into his playroom. Andy worked a lot of overtime hours trying to get Beady Eye's accounting books updated and back in order. Rex and Theresa worked together on one of her ongoing studio projects.

As promised, Pam returned for the remainder of her belongings. She and Rex were civil toward each other although both were uncomfortable with the situation. After Pam left for the final time, Rex took stock of what remained and decided on what he wanted to keep. The rest he would give to charity.

For the first time since her rehab, Lily spent time alone. Rex had given her strict instructions to call him whenever she needed anything or was having a bad day. He phoned her daily to check on her and she appreciated that. She loved hearing his voice and missed him terribly, but she refused to see him. It was difficult enough resisting the temptation without being close to him. Instead, she spent her time painting. It had been a very long time since she painted and was concerned about wanting to drink while doing it. It used to be her favorite pastime and she used to drink heavily while painting. This time, however, she was pleasantly surprised that while letting her creativity flow once again, she found herself satisfied with her talents and realized that she enjoyed it much more while sober. She was very proud of herself for battling her addictions and dealing with her temptations when she did feel them creeping into her day. She tackled each one individually and alone and was completely successful.

Theresa asked Lily to participate in her studio project, but Lily declined. She was reconsidering her life as a performer although kept it to herself. Andy kept her secret regarding her confession about wanting to become a councilor. She realized that she had a newfound friend in someone that had always been there for her. She just didn't see it until now. She and Andy spent some time together when he could get away from the office.

Theresa was finishing her studio project and she and Rex were in the studio together for the final session. It was raining heavily but it did not dampen their spirits as they recorded the final takes. Every one involved in the project listened to the final mixes and they all voiced their approval. There was a dinner party to celebrate. Theresa didn't want to go.

"I have a bus to catch," Theresa explained.

"Why are you taking a bus?" Rex asked.

"My car is in the repair shop again and Jake doesn't get off work until six o'clock. I want to go home and relieve the babysitter. I miss being with my kids. Leaving them behind all the time is why I hate touring. I promised my family that I wouldn't go away again and they were disappointed when I rejoined Threshold. They were understanding and forgiving, but it was still hard to do."

"I know Lily really appreciated you stepping up to the plate for her. We all feel that it was above and beyond your duty to stay on when she returned."

"It's been fun," Theresa confessed. "Performing gets into your blood. Lily isn't the only one battling addictions."

"Come on," Rex said. "I'll drive you home."

"Thanks, but I need to run some errands. You go to the dinner party."

"I don't feel like partying. I'd rather help a good friend in the rain. I'll take you wherever you need to go."

Theresa put on her rain jacket and covered her head and face with the hood. Rex grabbed her hand and they laughed as they ran together to Rex's car. He unlocked the doors with the remote and opened the door for her. After she was in, he closed her door and ran around to his side. The windows quickly steamed up from the moisture and the defrosters still hadn't cleared them completely when Rex pulled out of the parking lot. He drove her to the bank so she could pay some bills.

"It's across the street," Rex noticed. "Do you want me to turn around so you're closer?"

"No, thanks. I'll just dash across the street. A little water won't kill me."

Once again, Theresa pulled her hood up over her head and got out of the car. At a break in the traffic flow, she began to run across the street. Suddenly, a dark blue sedan raced down the street at a high speed. It slammed into Theresa, sending her several feet into the air. The sedan did not slow down and sped around a corner, out of sight.

"Theresa!" Rex shouted.

Rex was the first one to reach Theresa's crumpled unconscious body on the road. Several others quickly gathered and all traffic stopped in both directions.

"Someone call nine-one-one!" Rex ordered.

Rain dripped off his face and mixed with his tears. He held Theresa's head in his lap and tried to shelter her from the rain. Some bystanders held their umbrellas over them and someone brought a blanket. The water quickly mixed with the blood and soaked the blanket and their clothes. It seemed an eternity before the emergency personnel arrived and began doing their jobs.

Rex rode in the ambulance with Theresa. At the hospital, doctors treated him for shock while the trauma teams cared for Theresa. Once again, the entire Threshold family slowly filtered in to support each other and wait for information. Jake arrived with their two children in tow. The woman that had replaced Tony as crew leader, Patty Davenport, took the children to the cafeteria to distract them from what was happening to their mother.

After Rex was treated, the hospital gave him clothes and the police collected his wet clothing as evidence because Theresa's blood was on it. He gave a statement to the officers as best as he could recall. They were also questioning everyone else that was on the scene as witnesses.

"I was so horrified," Rex said, "that I didn't even think to get a plate number or anything. It just all happened so fast. I was adjusting the defroster and only looked up after I heard the impact." He shuddered. "I still don't really know what happened."

Cindy arrived at the hospital and after a short stay, took Theresa's children home with her. No one could reach Mike in Mexico and everyone felt his absence. Everyone else did their best to comfort Jake. After several hours in surgery, the doctor came down to the waiting family. He addressed Jake while everyone else listened.

"Your wife has some very serious internal injuries. We've controlled the bleeding and are monitoring her closely. Both of her legs are broken in several places. She will require several surgeries and extensive physiotherapy to help her to walk again. We do believe she will walk again. She also has a skull fracture but her brain wave patterns are fine. We won't know for several more days if there will be any permanent neurological damage, but she is stable and she should recover. She is still in critical condition but we'll know more within the next forty-eight hours. I think she's incredibly lucky to be alive. She's very strong."

"Can I see her?" Jake asked.

"Yes, just be forewarned that she is still unconscious and very badly banged up."

After Jake left with the doctor, the remaining Threshold family asked Rex about the accident. He answered their questions as best as he could.

"I don't want to appear shallow," Peter began, "but what happens to Threshold now? What do we do for the rest of the tour?"

Benjamin once again took charge of the situation. "I can only assume that Theresa will want us to continue on as originally planned. She was only supposed to be a temporary fill-in for Lily so could focus on her family and her other projects. This is devastating but we have to give our fans the best we can and carrying on without Theresa will be difficult but will be healing for not only us, but also her fans. The tour will continue as planned. As soon as Mike returns, you'll need to go over your material and adjust it accordingly."

"It just seems like we're jinxed," Andy said. "Why are terrible things happening to our beautiful women?"

Andy's statement made Lily's stomach churn and her skin feel cold.

Within twenty-four hours, the police located the car that struck Theresa in an abandoned warehouse parking lot. The rain washed a lot of evidence away but the damage on the front grill and hood of the car was consistent with striking a person. There was blood trapped inside the grill. The DNA was a perfect match to Theresa. The police also found the owner and presumed driver of the sedan slumped over in the driver's seat and they assumed he was drunk. The police demanded that he get out of the car. When he didn't respond, they drew their guns. Upon opening the driver's door, they discovered that the driver had been murdered.

Chapter Twenty-Eight

Mike and Cora cut their vacation short and returned to Chicago as soon as they heard about Theresa's accident. Theresa regained consciousness and miraculously began to recover. She was defeating all odds and had a good chance at a full recovery.

Threshold went into the rehearsal stage as soon as Mike returned. It didn't take very long to rework the material and fill in the gaps that Theresa was leaving. They performed with a heavy heart but were optimistic with Theresa's strength and good spirits. She reminded them that she was going to leave Threshold soon anyway.

The day quickly arrived when the band and crew had to leave home to continue the tour. They left reluctantly but fans' letters of encouragement uplifted their spirits. The months of July and August took them through Memphis, Tennessee; Atlanta, Georgia; Miami, Florida; Charlotte, North Carolina; Baltimore, Maryland and Syracuse, New York.

In the heat of August, they left New York State and drove once again into Canada. This time they were going to Montreal, Quebec then east to Halifax, Nova Scotia. After Halifax, they only had one more show and that was in Boston, Massachusetts. Lily felt nervous about being in Quebec again. Her stress level increased as she worried about running into reminders of the family and home that had been taken from her so violently. To try to divert her thoughts she began practicing her French.

When they arrived in Montreal, there was a huge outpouring of affection. Rex was the only one who knew of Lily's connection to the French-Canadian province so he kept a watchful eye on her for signs of stress or any other problems that may have surfaced.

The concert was a complete sell-out. Canadian fans seemed to have traveled from areas miles and even provinces away. They expected the same response in Halifax. Everyone was having a great time and the response of the fans was deafening. It was exhilarating but also exhausting.

After the concert, they all retired to their dressing rooms for showers and a change of clothes. Lily found herself alone in her dressing room and suddenly felt lonely for Theresa. She hadn't realized how much she cared about Theresa and sharing girl talk after the shows. She was packing away the last of her belongings when there was a knock at her door. She opened it, expecting Andy. She was startled to see a security guard.

"Excuse me, Miss Rose," the guard said in a thick French accent. "May I speak with you?"

"Sure," Lily answered. "What can I do for you?"

Lily was expecting a request for some autographs. Instead, his words concerned her.

"There is an elderly gentleman at the side entrance that claims to be your grandfather. We have strict orders not to allow anyone access to you under any circumstances, but this man seems to be genuinely sincere. He insists that you're his granddaughter." The guard leaned in to whisper. "He said that he would pay me to ask you if you would see him. I refused the money, but am doing as he requested."

Lily paled noticeably. "Did he give you his name?"

"Oui," he answered in French. "He said that his name was Pierre Edwards and you were his Manon."

Lily felt weak and her knees trembled. She reached for the doorframe for support.

"Are you alright?" the guard asked.

"Yes, I'm fine. My grandfather's name is Pierre."

Lily pondered what to do for a few minutes. She made a decision.

"Escort him back here. I'll see him but you do not leave him alone with me. Do you understand?"

"Oui."

The guard left and Lily sat in a nearby chair, leaving the door opened. She was flooded with childhood memories and wondered if she really did have living family. A few minutes later, the guard returned with a man in his late seventies.

"Manon?" Pierre asked.

"Yes."

"Est cela vraiment vous?"

"Forgive me. Mon français n'est bon plus. My French is not good anymore."

Pierre approached her, reached out, and took both of her hands.

"You look just like your father!" Pierre exclaimed in broken English. He began to cry. "I thought you were lost forever! I can't believe I'm looking at you and touching you."

"How did you find me?" Lily asked.

"A very nice young man came to my house. He introduced himself as a newspaper reporter from Montreal. He said that he recognized you from your band picture. He went to school with you when you were both very young. He knew how to find me and wanted to do a story on how it felt to have a famous American granddaughter from such a small place in Quebec.

"I told him that you had been lost to us as a child. I had no idea where you were. I was shocked to find out that you had changed your name and was famous."

With the security guard still listening, Lily interrupted him.

"Excuse me, Papa."

Lily turned to the guard and addressed him.

"It's alright. Merci. Wait outside the room, s'il vous plaît."

After the guard closed the door, Lily offered her grandfather a seat.

"I'm sorry. Please continue."

"I did not know what to do. I am an old man. I have a bad heart. He was offering to photograph our reunion for his story, but I did not want that. If I was to reunite with my lost granddaughter, I did not want strangers recording the event. I explained to him that I had limited means and could use his money for the story, but not at the expense of my family.

"He felt compassion and said that it broke his heart that a family should be lost to one another. He bought me a train ticket to come here. He gave me money to buy new clothes and stay in a nice motel. He told me to keep whatever was extra and that I might need to bribe someone to let me see you. I did not know if it would work, but I had to try. I had to know that it was really you and that you were all right.

"We looked for you for years. After your mother left, we got a card for a few Christmases. No other letters or photos came. Then the cards stopped and any letters that we sent were returned to us. Someone told your grandmother that your mother remarried and we didn't know her new name. We lost touch and did not know what to do.

"Your father was our only child and you and your brother were our only grandchildren. Our hearts ached for years and we held out hope that someday we would find you again. Poor Nana died a long time ago. I wish I could share this moment with her.

"You are so incredibly beautiful. You always were as a child and I am a proud old man to see you like this. Your mother must be proud as well. How is she?"

Lily had remained quiet until this question. She was confused with the discovery of her grandfather and his question about her mother brought many terrible reminders of the life she had lived and hidden. This sudden and unwelcome invasion of her past into her present was most likely inevitable but she had hoped that it would never occur.

"My mother died a long time ago."

"Oh, I'm so sorry. She was so young. What about Donny and the man who became your father?"

"He wasn't much of a father and they're both dead too."

"What? They are all dead?"

"They all died within several months of each other."

"What happened? Where did you go? How did you manage? You were just a child!"

"It's a part of my life that I left behind a very long time ago and I'm not willing to discuss it."

Obviously curious and disappointed, Pierre respected her wishes and did not question her further about it.

"Tell about yourself then. You are very talented and successful with this music. Are you happy? Do you have a family of your own, a nice young man at least?"

Lily smiled. "I'm very happy, healthy and strong. I have a great life and this band is my family now. With all the touring we do, I haven't had time to establish myself in a lasting relationship. Some of these guys manage, but it's not easy."

"I'm so glad that reporter found me and brought us together. Some things are fated to be! Do you have time to come away with me and talk some more? I want to know you. We were close when you were a child, but I don't know this beautiful woman that you've grown into."

"No, I'm sorry. We have to leave soon. Actually, they're all probably waiting for me. We're going to Halifax by bus and it's a long drive."

"How can I find you again? Please give me your address and phone number so that I don't lose you again. You are the last of my family and I thought until now that I was alone."

A knock at the door interrupted their conversation. It opened without hesitation and Andy walked in. He was surprised to find that Lily was not alone.

"Lily, we're waiting for you. We're ready to go. Is everything all right? Why is there a security guard outside? Who are you?" Andy addressed Pierre.

"I'll explain later. I'll be along in a moment."

Andy scrutinized her and the man with her.

"Is everything alright?" Andy repeated.

"Everything's fine. I'll be right there. Could you take my bags for me?"

Andy picked up her bags and reluctantly turned to leave. He stopped and looked back. Lily gave him a gentle push and smiled.

"I'm all right. Go."

Andy hesitated outside but Lily closed the door.

"I really need to leave. They're waiting for me."

"I need to know how to find you."

Lily grabbed the notepad and pen that was on the makeup table and handed it to him.

"Here, give me your information and I'll contact you as soon as possible."

Pierre wrote his address and phone number in a weak scribble. He handed it to her.

"My eyesight isn't very good, but I can read ok. Please, don't wait too long. It's already been too long."

Lily opened the door and motioned to the guard. Andy had disappeared with her bags.

"Please escort my visitor out and take good care of him. See if you can get him a taxi back to his hotel."

She turned to her grandfather.

"Thank you for finding me. I'll call as soon as I can. Take care of yourself."

"If I see your reporter friend, I'll tell him that I found you and that we had a lovely visit. He said that he would come back to see me. He must have been a good friend to care so much about you."

"I'm not sure who it could be. I haven't stayed in touch with anyone."

"He told me that the two of you were friends and that he missed you terribly. He was going to stop in and visit you soon. His name was Ricky."

Chapter Twenty-Nine

It was very late at night and almost everyone was asleep on board the Threshold tour bus. The driver drove carefully along the dark Trans-Canada highway through Quebec and into New Brunswick. It would take the bus several hours to get to Halifax then they would have the night to relax before they had to make scheduled appearances and interviews before the concert the following day. After that, they would travel to Boston, Massachusetts for their final concert of this tour. They were all exhausted and anxious to get back home and resume some normalcy to their lives. People think that the lifestyle of a touring band is glamorous. Anyone who has lived it would quickly correct them.

Lily was still awake, staring out the window into the darkened countryside. As exciting as it was to reunite with her estranged grandfather, the fact remained that a terror from her past arranged it. That terrified her. She never imagined that she would ever again interact with her flesh and blood family. The circumstances surrounding this reunion left her greatly disturbed.

Memories of her family flooded back to her. The last time she had seen Pierre was two months after her father's funeral. Pierre came to their house as her mother was packing the last of their belongings into an old, beaten rental van. She sold most of the furniture and appliances. She took what remained and went back to Milwaukee to begin a new life. Her mother had promised Pierre in her broken French that she would stay in touch and continue to keep him involved in his grandchildren's lives.

Lily's entire life began to play out along the dark highway. She felt all the losses, sorrow, pain and fear that had encompassed her life. She thought of Jackson and the house that she loved which now belonged to Peter and Cindy. She thought of Theresa's broken body mending slowly and painfully. She remembered the brutality of Ricky who was seeking her out and possibly waiting for her. The federal agents warned her about her public life putting her at risk again.

Lily cried quietly. She considered waking Rex and sharing her fears about Ricky's contact with Pierre. That would mean discussing some emotions that were too intense for her to even deal with herself. An influx of issues bombarded her. She now realized that she had never dealt with many things despite Corona's best efforts. The memories were pounding in her head and her anxiety reached a point that was unbearable. She needed to get off the bus and get some air.

Somewhere in New Brunswick, Lily fell into a fitful sleep. Nightmares haunted her during her sleep and nightmares that were more real haunted her when she was awake. She dozed sporadically during the entire trip to Halifax. Andy wanted to ask her about her visitor but she was unapproachable.

After several stops, the bus pulled into their Halifax hotel around four o'clock in the afternoon. The city was beautiful and had an incredible fortress that overlooked the harbor. They realized that their hotel on the waterfront was within walking distance of many shops and tourist attractions. They were excited to shower and check out the nightlife after they had decent meals.

Around seven o'clock in the evening, some of the members started to meet for socializing. Rex and Mike were in the hotel lounge having coffee when Andy came in.

"Have you guys seen Lily?" Andy asked.

"No," said Rex. "She told me that she was going to sleep for awhile. She didn't get any sleep on the bus so she was going to have dinner, a bath and go to bed."

"I just knocked at her door. She's not answering. I tried calling her on the room phone then her cell phone and she's not answering those either. I'm a little worried about her after what happened in Montreal."

Rex immediately became concerned.

"What happened in Montreal?" Rex asked.

"I thought she might have told you about it. I went to get her because she was taking so long and I found her in her dressing room with some old guy. She was pale and looked upset, but she sent me away. There was a security guard hanging around outside her room too. I don't know who they were. When I asked her about it on the bus, she told me that she didn't want to talk about it and she sent me away again."

Rex put money on the bar and left the lounge. The other two men followed him to Lily's room. Rex pounded on the door.

"Lily! Are you in there? Open up. It's Rex. Andy, did you confirm there was no wet bar in this room?"

"After what happened in Houston, I have made absolutely certain that I personally check each room before she goes in."

When there was no answer, Andy went to get security to open her room. When they arrived with a master key, they opened the door only to find that Lily was not in the room at all. Her unopened bags were on the bed. Her cellular phone was on the nightstand.

"This is a big city," said Mike. "She could be anywhere. Does she know Halifax at all?"

"I don't think so," Rex answered. "This just isn't like her to disappear. Let's get as many of us together as possible and organize a search of the immediate area. We'll check restaurants, bars, stores, whatever's open. She might just want to be alone for a while and may be out on that cute tugboat, but I have a bad feeling about this. She's been at the breaking point for awhile and if something happened in Montreal…"

Rex didn't continue the sentence that would have referred to Quebec as her home.

They went back to the hotel and gathered the band, crew and drivers. Rex got a map and each person took an area to search. One of the crew noticed something on the map.

"There's a ferry service that crosses the water into Dartmouth. She might have gone over on that."

Rex sighed, "Let's search this area first. If we can't find her, we'll widen the search. My phone is on. Call me the minute anyone finds anything and check in frequently in case one of us finds her. There's no sense in running around foolishly. Let's go!"

They all dispersed to their designated search areas. After thirty-five minutes, Rex's phone rang.

"This is Rex," he said into the phone.

"I found her!"

"Great! Who is this?"

"It's Janice," the voice said. Janice Johnston was their head lighting technician. "She's been drinking for quite awhile by the looks of things."

Janice told Rex where she was. Rex gave her instructions to stay with Lily and to try to stop her from drinking anymore. Rex phoned Mike and Andy and told them to call everyone else while he went to retrieve Lily. He quickly found the bar and saw Lily fighting with Janice, who had taken her drink away.

"I wasn't finished with that!" Lily slurred.

"Yes, you are," Janice said gently.

"Thanks," Rex said as she stepped between her and Lily. Lily was trying to get her drink back and was hitting at Janice to accomplish that goal.

"Oh!" exclaimed Lily. "Here comes the cavalry! My knight in shining amour has come to rescue me."

Rex chose to release his anger on the bartender.

"Don't you know who this is?" Rex demanded.

"A pretty girl with a credit card," the bartender answered.

"Give me her card back. She's done."

The bartender gave Rex Lily's credit card. Rex and Janice needed to get her out in fresh air and try to walk the inebriation off.

"Come on," Rex said as he put his arm around her. "We're going for a walk."

Rex helped her to stand while Janice gathered Lily's purse and jacket. Between the two sober friends, they managed to get Lily out of the bar and staggered outside.

"Oh, Janice!" Lily continued to slur her words. "Are you coming with us? We could have a threesome!"

They managed to walk a few blocks with several stumbles from Lily.

"Look!" Lily stopped suddenly and pointed. "There's water! I want to see boats!"

They walked toward Halifax's harbor in the cool evening air. The ships at the dock were silent except for the gentle lapping of the water against their hulls.

The water was still and beautifully reflected the city lights that were starting to twinkle in the twilight hours. It was very quiet and serene and there were quite a few people strolling along the boardwalks. Lily was babbling incoherently while music from nearby restaurants drifted along in the air. They found a bench and managed to get Lily to sit between them, her head bobbing.

"Does she speak French?" Janice asked. "It sounds like she's speaking French."

"That's possible," Rex answered. "She used to speak it. Montreal must have been bad for her. Please don't repeat anything you learn about her tonight."

"You have my word," Janice promised.

Suddenly, Lily lifted her head and looked at Janice.

"I don't know you! I don't speak to you enough. Oh, I've been such a snob. You have a very important job and I've ignored you. That was very rude of me. Please forgive me!"

"There's nothing to forgive. We are all busy with our responsibilities."

"But, I only get on stage and sing. You make all the lights twinkle and blink. That's so cool. Can we switch places? I want to make the pretty lights sparkle. You can sing!"

"That's alright. I like what I do."

"But you're so beautiful! Rex, don't you think she's beautiful? She's much prettier than I am. She can probably sing better too."

"I'm not a singer," Janice answered.

"Neither am I!" Lily insisted. "I just pretend. I've got all of you fooled, don't I?"

Rex remained quiet. It had been so long since Lily had been drinking, she seemed out of control. He didn't want to think what she would have done before the night was over if they hadn't found her. Even when she was drinking all the time, she never acted like this.

"Rex!" Lily demanded. "Tell Janice how pretty she is! Janice, don't you think Rex is handsome? Sexy, Rexy!"

"That's enough," Rex said gently.

"You're both beautiful. You'd make a lovely couple. Since I've cut you off, maybe she'll sleep with you, Rex."

Janice's jaw hung open, not believing what she was hearing.

"Lily!" Rex said sternly. "You are drunk and you don't know what you're saying."

"Oh, pooh," Lily said, dismissing him with a wave of her hand. She turned back to Janice. "He's very sweet you know. And gentle. I've been with a lot of men and none were as gentle and as loving as he was. I kind of regret ending it. I miss him so much!"

Janice and Rex stared at each other. Both were speechless. Janice smiled and put her hands on Lily's shoulders.

"Gee, you've been speaking in French all evening. I'm sorry but I don't understand a thing you've been saying.

Janice looked over at Rex. "Do you understand French?"

"Uh, no. I don't."

"Well, I guess we'll never know what she's been babbling about, will we?"

"No, I guess not."

Rex forced a grateful smile. He didn't know Janice very well, but he appreciated what she was doing. Her feigning ignorance to Lily's outburst was beyond anything he could have expected or asked for. He just had to have faith that she would continue to keep their secret.

Chapter Thirty

"How is she?" Mike asked Rex.

Rex had just left Lily in her motel room under Janice's care. He had just rejoined Mike in the room that they were sharing.

"She was sleeping when I left. Actually, she passed out. Janice is going to stay with her for the night. She'll call if I'm needed."

Rex sat on the edge of his bed. He ran his hands over his face and through his hair. He sighed heavily, stood and began to pace. He was visibly agitated and upset. Mike knew that his friend was feeling frustrated and angry.

"Don't be angry at her," Mike told Rex.

"I'm not angry at her. I'm angry at myself."

"Why?"

"I let her down!"

"You did no such thing."

"Andy was the one who knew something had happened in Montreal. Andy was the one that knew she was upset. Andy was the one who noticed that she was missing. Maybe Andy should be her Support Buddy. I'm obviously not doing a good job."

"You're doing fine. She's been doing fine."

"That's just it. She was doing so well, I forgot that she had a problem. I got so complacent and confident in her efforts that I got sloppy. I let her down."

"You've been there for her every step of the way."

"Not tonight. She went out and got stupid-drunk. I've seen her drunk a lot of times but she was never this bad."

"She's been sober a long time. Alcohol is going to affect her differently now. She's been doing incredibly well. Not many alcoholics can go for as long as she has without a fall off the wagon. She came close in Houston. Tonight was just too much for her to handle."

"I want to know what happened in Montreal to trigger this. It has to do with a visit from some old guy and I think it has to do with her past. Forgive me, but I know her past and I've been keeping her secrets. She should have been able to come to me with this."

"You're not her keeper."

"No, but I'm her friend. I'm supposed to be supporting her."

"You have been supporting her more than anyone could have imagined or expected. You've sacrificed a lot of yourself for her. You've been there every time she called. You can't control her. She made a choice tonight. She decided not to involve you. If that bothers you, tough. She has her own life and you can't care more about her than she does herself. If she wanted to come to you, she would have. She's come to you every time before and she will again. Something personal happened to her that she just needed to run away and hide for a while. When she's sober again, you two can talk and work things out. She must be accountable to herself. You need to step back and let her live her own life. You're too obsessed with her."

"I'm not obsessed with her. I've been trying to help her."

"When Lily came out of rehab, you helped her every step of the way. We all did. We know what you went through with Rachael and we cut you a lot of slack. Nevertheless, you've gone way beyond helping her now. You are obsessed and your entire life revolves around her."

"It does not."

"I've known you for more than twenty years. I know that you're in love with Lily."

Rex stopped pacing and sat down again on the edge of the bed, facing Mike who was still sitting on the edge of his bed.

Mike continued gently, "I saw it that first day she walked into Beady Eye. We were all enamored with her and we all felt like big brothers to her. There was something tough but vulnerable about her. She was beautiful and confident, but mysterious and frightened all at the same time. She shocked us all when she agreed to come on board with Threshold. We all settled into that protective role around her, but it's gone beyond that for you, hasn't it? You spend a lot of time alone with her. We all noticed it, but no one's going to say anything. But I'm saying something now."

"What do you want me to say?" asked Rex.

"I want you to be honest with me. I'm not tiptoeing around you anymore in regards to this. We're having this conversation now whether you want to or not."

"Look, I've got divided loyalties. You've been my friend forever. You're like a brother to me. I care about what you're going through and I'd be fine with this except that you're married to my sister. I need to think about what Pam's going through at home. She's not stupid either."

"When was the last time you talked to Pam?"

"I haven't actually talked to her in months. She always seems to be in New York."

"That's because she lives there."

Rex filled Mike in on the details of their divorce.

....

Janice let Rex into Lily's room.

"She's in the bathroom," Janice told him.

Rex went into the bathroom and found Lily sitting on the floor in a crumpled heap and resting her head on the toilet.

"Go away," Lily murmured.

"No, I won't," Rex said gently. "Can you get up?"

"No. I don't want to."

"Are you sick?"

"Yes, I'm sick. I'm a sick alcoholic."

"I mean, are you still vomiting?"

"Not for awhile."

Rex reached for a clean washcloth and ran it under cold water. After ringing out the access water, he laid it on the back of her neck.

"Go away," Lily repeated.

"No."

"You can't help me anymore. There's no point."

Rex sat next to her on the floor.

"You slipped up last night. That's all right. You're allowed to make mistakes. Everyone does. You're very strong. You're a fighter and a survivor. You can get through this. Let me help."

"Do I have to go back to rehab?"

"No. You went on a binge. You may want to get some more counseling, but I don't think your problem is the booze."

"My problems will be with me as long as I live. They will never go away."

Lily turned her head to look at Rex, but her eyes closed and she moaned.

"Let me help you get back to the bed. You'd be more comfortable there. I know that I'm not comfortable sitting on this floor."

Rex removed the cloth from Lily's neck and placed it in the sink. Janice had been waiting. She moved in to help Rex lift Lily off the floor and guided her back to bed.

"Oh, I'm dizzy," complained Lily. "My hair hurts. Can you turn off the sun?"

After Lily was on the bed, Janice closed the window curtains to block the sun. She then went and returned with the washcloth that she rinsed with hot water. She returned and washed Lily's face.

"Oh," moaned Lily. "That feels nice. Thanks."

"Janice," Rex addressed her, "go and get some sleep. I'd like to talk to Lily for awhile."

"Sure." Janice removed the cloth from Lily's face. "Rex will take over now. I'll be back in awhile."

"Thanks," Lily repeated.

Janice left while Rex made Lily comfortable.

"Do you want to talk about it?" Rex asked as he sat on the edge of the bed next to her.

Lily shook her head from side to side, which caused her to wince in pain.

"I know something happened in Montreal," Rex continued. "I want to help you and take care of you. I can't do that unless you choose to come to me. We're all concerned and Andy told us about the old man in your dressing room. Who is he?"

"His name is Pierre Edwards."

"Edwards?"

"He's my dad's father."

"Your grandfather! You said that your whole family was dead."

"That's what I thought."

"How did he find you?"

Lily began to cry. It was apparent that every move she made caused her great pain and effort. Rex lay down next to her and held her.

"It's okay. I'm here."

"I didn't have to be alone. All that time I was in trouble, I had grandparents that were looking for me. I could have gone home and they would have looked after me. All this for nothing. I was living on the streets and selling myself and I had a family that would have loved me!"

"We can't change the past. What's important is that he found you. You can start over."

"It's too late for that."

"Why?"

"Because I loved him."

"I don't understand."

"I know you don't. You never will."

"I want to."

"You can't protect me anymore. I have to leave again."

"What do you mean?"

"Look at my life! I've been living in a fantasy. I told you a long time ago that my life is a façade. I look around at everyone I've fooled into caring about me. I've been lying to everyone, including myself that I'm something special. All I am is a big fraud. My friends and fans think I'm someone I'm not. I can't continue this charade!"

"Your life is not a charade. Everyone changes and you are a very real person. You are an amazing person. You are a natural performer who cares very much about her music and her fans. You were born to do this. Many celebrities use alternate names and very few reveal their private lives to protect themselves from the public eye. That's all you've done.

"As far as your friends and fans go, you haven't fooled anyone. You had the opportunity to start over and became the person you wanted to be. Many people would love that chance. You've put your ugly past behind you and rose above it. I don't think many people could have endured half of what you have and survived, let alone have the personal and professional success you have. Not many and stay sane, that is."

"Sane?" Lily laughed and immediately winced again. "I'm hardly sane anymore. I've forgotten who I really am. If I were sane, I would have stayed in my quiet little world in my beautiful house with Jackson. No, I had to go to that stupid bar and start singing. Then I couldn't just do that. I had to become a high-profile singer with a target on my head."

"Why are you talking that way?"

"Ricky's found me! He's the one who gave money to my grandfather and told me where to find me! The FBI told me that I was being stupid. Now I can't even go back to them for protection. They've wiped their hands of me and I have nowhere to go! I can't go back to Chicago. He's waiting for me. I will never know when he's going to get me. He wants me dead. He tried years ago and he's going to try again.

"I'm sorry but I need to leave now. I need to go somewhere else where he can't find me. I just need to disappear. The tabloids will have a field day and everyone will worry, but they'll just have to get over it. I can stay here in Canada somewhere or maybe go to Europe. I'm not as well known over there."

"Please don't do anything hasty. We'll work through this. We'll get the police involved…"

"You know as well as I do that won't help. The police can't do anything until he makes a move and then it will be too late. Instead, they'll be investigating my murder."

"Then we'll hire more personal bodyguards. Please. Don't go away. I need you."

"I can't do this anymore. I can't live out of a suitcase anymore. I need a safe and secure home to go to everyday. This lifestyle isn't for me. I thought it would be fun and at first, it was. Now, I just want it to end."

"Can you hold out for two more shows? We'll do Halifax tonight, then we go to Boston and then we're done. Please, hold on for just a few more days. I'll help you through it."

"I don't think I can."

Rex held Lily tight as they lay in bed together. He kissed her on the forehead then the nose. Carefully he kissed her lips.

"I love you. More than that. I'm in love with you. I don't know anything else about the future except that I want you in it."

"I don't have the strength."

"Pam and I have divorced."

Silence hit the room as loudly as if a bomb had detonated in it.

"What?" asked Lily, disbelieving her ears.

"Pam transferred her company to New York and bought an apartment there. Our divorce was finalized a few weeks ago."

"Why didn't you tell me?"

"We didn't tell anyone. We weren't quite sure how to handle it, so we handled it quietly. I didn't want you to know because I didn't want you to feel responsible or obligated to me."

"Am I responsible?"

"No. Our marriage was over a long time ago. We just didn't realize it until we both found something else that we loved more than each other. Our marriage was arranged for us and although we got along well and there we no major problems, it just wasn't real. Pam fell in love with her freedom and her company and I fell in love with you."

"I don't know what to say. I'm not sure I can handle this right now."

"I don't want you to make any decisions yet about anything. The first thing we need to do is get some food and aspirin into you and you get some sleep. We'll do the show tonight and then we'll go to Boston. When we get back to Chicago, we'll just take things one day at a time and see what happens."

Chapter Thirty-One

Lily managed to eat and sleep a little. She was extremely hung-over and shaky. Rex stayed with her all day trying to nurse her back to a condition that she would allow her to perform that evening. While she was sleeping, there was a knock at the door. Rex answered it quietly. Peter stood on the other side, holding his cellular phone.

"Hi," whispered Peter. "How's Lily?"

"She's better. She's resting, but she said that she'll be good to go tonight."

"That's terrific. Do you think she'd be up to talking on the phone? Cindy needs to talk to her."

Lily was awake and listening to them. "I'll talk to her," she said.

Peter entered the room and handed Lily his phone. Lily sat up and swung her legs over the edge of the bed.

"Thanks," Lily said. She spoke into the phone, "Hello Cindy."

"Hi Lil," Cindy said. "Are you alright? Peter told me what happened."

"Yes, I'm fine. Just a little setback."

"An important looking letter arrived at our house addressed to you and another woman from something called the Sûreté du Québec. Do you know what that is?"

"It's the Quebec Provincial Police."

"It's addressed to 'Lily Rose Delphinium slash Dora Manon Edwards'. Did you used to have a roommate here?"

"No. Go ahead and open it and read it to me."

Lily could hear the tearing of paper. After a few seconds, Cindy began to read.

"'Ms. Edwards...' Are you sure it's all right for me to read her mail?"

"Trust me. It's all right. Go ahead."

"'Ms. Edwards, we have attempted contact with you by other means but have been unable to reach you. Therefore, we are contacting you through the Postal Service.

"'We regret to inform you of the death of Pierre Edwards.' Is this someone close to you?"

"I didn't know him that well. Does it say anything else?"

"'The circumstances of his death are suspicious and are currently under investigation.' What's that supposed to mean?"

"I'm not sure."

"There's a name and phone number of the constable in charge for you to contact for further information. Do you want it?"

"Not now. We'll be home in a few days. I'll deal with it then."

"I'm sorry for your loss."

"Thanks. I'll give you back to Peter now. Give Kevin a hug for me."

"I will. Bye!"

Lily gave the phone back to Peter. He took it and left. Rex locked the door and sat down beside her. She looked upset.

"Is everything all right?"

"My grandfather's dead."

"Oh, no. I'm so sorry."

"I'm more scared than upset. The police say that it's suspicious. I'm wondering if Ricky brought my past back to me then took it away again. I feel like a mouse that a cat's been playing with, waiting for the right moment to kill it."

"We need to arrange more security."

Rex started to rise, but Lily pulled him back down.

"There's time for that. Just hold me. I'm terrified and my head's killing me."

Rex held her and massaged her neck and head just as the therapists taught him.

"When this tour is over," Rex said quietly, "let's go away somewhere, just the two of us. We'll go to Hawaii or Jamaica, somewhere hot and sunny. We can swim and surf or just lay in the sand with wonderful non-alcoholic fruit beverages. We can just relax and be ourselves. We can just let things happen naturally without any inhibitions at all. We can explore our relationship without any interruptions."

"I don't want to continue to endanger you. I've already endangered enough people as it is."

"I can take care of myself and I can take care of you. I can protect you."

"I don't want to think anymore. Besides, doesn't Threshold have a new recording project to think about?"

"We're thinking about it, but we're also thinking more about putting Threshold on the shelf for awhile."

"Really?"

"We're all tired. Andy's already resigned as our drummer. He's going insane trying to do this road stuff. He'd rather settle in his regular nine-to-five office job and reconnect with his kids."

"He mentioned that to me in Toronto," Lily added.

"I need time to recollect my thoughts and priorities. These past few months has really gotten me stirred up. I need to deal with my gains and losses and put my feelings in order. Mike and Cora want to have some more quality time together. Peter and Cindy are expecting another child. That's a secret though. You didn't hear it from me!"

"That's terrific!"

"I really don't know if I can completely give up my music. Theresa once said that it gets in your blood."

"I can understand that. I know that I'm an addict and addicts often replace one thing with another. I gave up heroin and started on the booze, painkillers and marijuana. I gave those things up and now get a high from standing on a stage in front of thousands of screaming fans. I'm scared of what I might turn to next."

"You can get addicted to me."

"If Ricky knows where I am, it's just a matter of time before he gets to me. I don't know if I'd be safe anywhere."

"I don't want to lose you."

"I either move away and stay alive or I stay in Chicago and die. Either way, you lose me. I should never have come out of hiding, but I can't change what I've done. I wouldn't change all of the experiences I've had over the past couple of years. I now have people that truly care about me in my life; people that I can trust. I got sober. How priceless is that? I've had experiences that most people only dream about. I also got to experience what love is all about. However, I've not only placed my life in danger, but the lives of those I care about."

Rex took Lily's hands in his.

"We don't have to end what we have. I want to be with you. Stay with me. What we have together can continue to grow."

"What is it exactly that we have?"

"Pure, true love that will never die."

"We might though."

....

Lily and Rex sat in her dressing room at the concert hall. Her headache persisted and would not go away. She was terrified and shaking and begged Rex for something to get her through the show. Rex wouldn't let her although secretly he wished he could have something as well to calm his nerves. He now had a sense of what Lily's life had been like for so long. Lily was convinced that she saw Ricky everywhere. Rex also wondered if he were out there somewhere, watching and waiting.

Everyone involved with Threshold was told that a threat had been made on Lily's life in Montreal. Mike knew there was more to it, but didn't ask any questions. Security was increased at the concert hall and that entailed searches of all ticket holders' bags and purses. Anything seen as a potential threat was confiscated. This confused and angered many fans and made the media curious.

After the opening act was finished, the crews quickly removed their equipment, leaving only Threshold's on stage. It was time for Threshold to take the stage. Rex hadn't left Lily's side the entire day and was worried about her state of mind. She was still pale and trembling and tears filled her eyes.

"I can't do this!" Lily cried. "Give me something. Anything!"

"I can't do that," Rex comforted her. "We are all right here with you. Security has been increased. There are police officers everywhere. No one will get close to you. You'll be safe."

"I'll never be safe as long as he's alive!"

There was a knock at Lily's door, which caused both her and Rex to jump. Rex unlocked and opened it to find Andy standing there.

"Is Lily alright?" Andy asked.

"No, she's terrified," Rex replied. "Come in."

Andy entered and gave Lily a hug.

"I don't blame you," Andy told Lily, "but I'm sure this threat is harmless. It's just some crazy fan. It's happened to all of us at one time or another but the first time it happens, it really is very scary. I know that doesn't ease your worry, but nothing will happen to you. The audience is getting restless. We need to go on. You can do this. We're all in this together."

Andy left with Rex and Lily reluctantly following. The stage was dark with only enough lights to show the markings on the stage for each performer to position themselves. When everyone was in position, Mike gave a 'thumb's up' signal to the stage monitor sound engineer who in turn let the main stage sound engineer and lighting technician know that they were ready.

A single spotlight shone on Mike as he started playing the introduction to their first song on the keyboards. Shortly after, Andy joined in on drums as lights illuminated him. Rex joined, then Peter. Finally, lights blinded Lily, as she was the last to join in. She jumped at the sudden brightness, but began to play her tambourine automatically.

The entire show felt like an eternity to Lily. She felt like a robot, playing without emotion and could sense the restlessness in the audience. Even though Rex and Mike were only a few feet away, she felt entirely alone in a spotlight with all eyes on her. "Ricky, Ricky, Ricky, Ricky," the percussion instruments in her hands seem to be saying through every song. She missed lyrics, sang off key, and was convinced that she ruined the entire show.

Finally, the concert was over and she ran off the stage quickly ahead of everyone else. She slammed her dressing room door and locked it, amazed to still be alive. Traditionally, the band would wait a few minutes then go back on stage for two more songs as an encore performance. These few minutes passed with the fans cheering for more.

The crowd chanted Threshold's name repeatedly. They were ready to go back on stage, but Lily did not reappear. Concerned, Rex went to her dressing room and knocked.

"Come on, Sweetie," Rex called out. "Just a couple more then we can get out of here."

There was no answer, so Rex knocked again. He tried the door and found it unlocked. Cautiously, he opened the door and looked in.

Lily was gone.

Chapter Thirty-Two

Rex was sick with worry but did not know what to do. Since her bags were gone, it was assumed that she left voluntarily. Police easily found the taxi driver that drove her from the concert hall to the Halifax International Airport just outside the city. Rex's own admissions of her fears and desire to disappear made it a moot issue for the police.

Rex attempted to call her cellular phone several times. Each time, the service provider stated that she was out of range. All he could do was hope that she was safe and that she knew what she was doing. He would have preferred to be at her side and surround her with everyone who cared about her and would protect her. He believed that they could have kept her safe.

Lily had panicked and ran outside with her suitcases. She got in the nearest waiting taxi and instructed him to take her to the airport. The driver had recognized her but she begged him to remain quiet about where she had gone. She said that there was a personal emergency and didn't want the media all over it. She gave him an extra hundred dollars to buy his silence.

Upon arrival at the airport, Lily purchased a ticket for the first flight to Chicago. Another taxi ride found her around the back of her apartment building. She felt safe there and dashed inside through the parking garage and up the stairs, avoiding all the main areas, hoping to remain unseen.

In the hallway outside of her apartment, Lily breathed a sigh of relief that she made it home safely. She found the keys in her purse and unlocked the door and two deadbolts. She pushed the door open and brought her suitcases into the entryway. After setting her bags down, she turned and locked all three locks. As she did this, she noticed a smell. It took her a few minutes to identify it as cigarette smoke. She assumed that there was a malfunction in the ventilation system and made a mental note to call maintenance in the morning. It was well past midnight; too late to call. She would tolerate it for one night.

Lily decided to make some tea and relax, now that she was safe at home. She went into the kitchen and froze. Fear gripped her insides and paralyzed her entire body and mind. There were several cigarette butts that had been extinguished in her kitchen sink. She tried to swallow the lump in her throat but found that she couldn't breathe. Her heart pounded loudly in her ears. Without moving from her place, she reached down and opened the drawer in which she kept her knives. As she moved her hand around, she discovered that her large chef knife was not there.

Lily's kitchen had her trapped. Her countertop opened into the darkened living room but the only entrance was several feet to the left. That was where the hallway was located as well as the door to the outside world.

Slowly, Lily looked up. Suddenly a flash of light came from a chair. She flinched as a flame moved slowly through the air. It lit Ricky's face as he lit a cigarette.

"Welcome home."

The match was blown out, darkening Ricky's face once again. Lily glanced to the left at her suitcases still lying in the hallway. She looked back at Ricky. Enough light flowed from the kitchen to show his outline in the chair. She tried to judge how quickly she could get away. She was terrified, while Ricky remained cool.

"I've been following your rise to fame," Ricky said with the cigarette dangling from his lips. "Who'd have thought that scrawny kid would grow up so nice."

Lily was still frozen to the spot, trying to think clearly and decide what to do. Her only phone sat in her purse which was also in the hallway. If she screamed, she may be heard but didn't know how Ricky would respond in the time help might come, if it came at all. Frustrated and scared, tears began to blur her vision.

"How did you get in here?" Lily asked in a raspy whisper.

"Friends in high places, or rather low places in this case," Ricky inhaled on his cigarette then took his time exhaling the smoke. "Your concierge and I go back a long ways. It turns out that he has a new wife and kid that he's particularly fond of. Imagine that. After a conversation about the health of his family, he agreed to let me in here."

"What do you want from me?" Lily choked out.

"I came to reclaim my property."

"I don't have anything that belongs to you!"

"Dora, my dear," Ricky sneered, "it's you that belong to me. Have you forgotten all that I did for you? I gave you a home. I took care of you."

"You tried to kill me!"

"Minor details. One mistake. I've missed you. I missed feeling your beautiful body under mine, how good you felt in my arms. Mind you, I had to go a few years without any of that. I suppose you know that I was incarcerated for awhile. Of course, I was really angry at you for that."

Lily slowly inched her way left. Rex noticed her movement and slowly stood up. She froze again when the kitchen light flashed on her missing knife, looming large in his hand. Ricky began to laugh as he played with the knife. He moved closer to where Lily stood but she remained frozen.

"I knew you had many talents but I didn't know singing was one of them. I'll bet Mike knows all your wonderful talents. Maybe all your friends do. Or do they even know what you really are? I told the tabloids all about you. They love a good story and pay quite well for them. Alas, they never seem to be taken seriously as a reliable source of information, do they?"

"Just get out. I won't tell anyone you were here. Just leave me alone."

"I don't think so. I spent a lot of time and effort to get here. You belong to me. You sold me your soul a long time ago. Don't you remember?"

"No."

"You exchanged your soul for every fix I gave you."

"I'm clean now."

"I don't think you'll be singing that song when I'm through with you. I'll have you begging me to take care of you once again. Come on, don't make this so difficult. I'm not leaving until I get what I came for!"

Lily ran to the door, tripping over a suitcase. She partially regained her balance and grabbed the bag. She turned and swung it at Ricky who was upon her with the knife. The bag hit him which flung the knife from his hand. She used the distraction to grasp at the locks which were supposed to keep her safe, only now endangered her further.

Ricky grabbed Lily and attempted to wrap his arm around her neck. Instinctively, she turned her head so that her throat fell into the inside of his elbow, not allowing him to do any damage. Her nails dug into his arms. She could still smell the cigarette, but no longer knew where it was.

"I'm not leaving," he rasped into her ear.

Ricky realized he couldn't squeeze her neck so he spun her around, grabbing her arm. He pushed her face first into the wall and twisted her arm behind her back. She let out a yelp of pain.

"I could break your arm so you can't play your little jingle bell things."

Once again, he spun her around and slammed the back of her head against the wall that her face had just been against. His hand closed around her throat and he began to squeeze.

"Or I could crush your throat so you can't sing."

Lily was crying and choking, gasping for air. She was dizzy and once again, her vision blurred. Ricky leaned into her face, cigarettes on his breath and rage in his eyes. He loosened his hand slightly.

"You're a hard person to kill. Harder than others, that's for sure."

"Why did you have to kill Papa?" Lily gasped.

"I just used an extra pillow to make him sleep a little more comfortably. I would say that you were like a cat with nine lives, but I'm afraid that analogy wouldn't work either, seeing how your cat didn't have that many.

"Now, the MacKenzie woman. Actually, she was a mistake. I couldn't be in two places at once. I was a good model citizen, sitting with my parole officer when that happened. Stupid kid followed the guitar player. Never hire a boy to do a man's job. I hear she's going to be fine eventually. Unfortunately, the kid wasn't so lucky."

Ricky began to drag Lily down the hall, still squeezing her throat.

"You have a nice place here. The bed is very comfortable. Let's check it out, shall we? How about something to help us relax first?"

"No!"

Tears fell down Lily's face as she struggled. With her vision still blurred, she kicked and scratched at him but to no avail.

"I like you feisty."

The phone in Lily's purse had been ringing, but never acknowledged. Ricky pushed her down onto the bed. As she landed, she somersaulted and grabbed the bedside lamp. She threw it at him and it bounced off his arm. He caught it by the cord and quickly wrapped it around her throat, tightening it. She clawed at it but began to lose consciousness. She continued to try to struggle, but her strength was fading fast.

Ricky released the cord and threw the lamp across the room. He pinned her down by sitting with his full weight on her chest.

"Please don't," Lily begged, barely audible.

"Shut up!"

Ricky struck her across the face.

"I own you!"

Lily begn to pass out from the pain and shortness of breath. From somewhere, she could feel rubber tubing being tied around her arm. She always knew she'd die because of her addictions, but not like this. She felt the needle begin to slide into her arm. Suddenly she was hallucinating. A dark, ghostly image flew across the room and a sudden lightness overcame her body. She took a final deep breath and mercifully sank into the welcome darkness that beckoned her.

Chapter Thirty-Three

Lily began to hear things. There was a terrible pain in her head and her eyes didn't want to open. The noises were both distant and close. She couldn't make out what the noises were despite the fact that they were familiar. She couldn't understand what the voices were saying. She could feel things touching her but couldn't move. She wanted to slip back into unconsciousness, but something was keeping her awake. She tried to quiet her mind and figure out where she was. Then she remembered.

Lily felt the needle in her arm. She screamed and grabbed the needle and began to pull it out. Ricky grabbed her arm and told her to stop. She fought him and struggled against him as he once again pushed down on her.

Lily heard her name repeatedly.

"Lily, Lily, Lily…"

Ricky never called her Lily. She was confused. She stopped struggling and looked around her. Her head began to clear a bit but she had trouble focusing her eyes and could only make out shapes and blurred images.

Lily was in a hospital again. Those were the familiar sounds. She hated them but they were somehow comforting.

"It's alright. You're safe." She recognized Rex's voice.

"Rex?" Lily began to cry. "Rex!"

Rex held her and let her cry. A nurse reinserted the intravenous catheter that Lily had pulled out as Rex explained where she was and what was happening.

"Why can't I see?"

"Those fragments shifted in your brain and it's affecting your eyesight."

"I'm blind!"

"The best surgeons and specialists are here and they are going to do everything they can to fix you as good as new. Dr. Powell is going to make you better than before."

"What if I'm not? What if I'm blind forever? What if I don't wake up again?"

"You have defeated the odds your whole life. The worst is now over. You don't have anything else to worry about except to get better again. You've done it before. You'll do it again."

"What if I don't?"

"We'll take things as they come, together."

"How did I get here?" Lily sobbed.

"Everyone makes choices and mistakes that lead us down paths, for better or worse. Those paths eventually bring us to a good place in the end. That's where you are now and I'm here to be with you."

"No, I mean, how did I get here, in this hospital? How long have I been here? How did you find me here?"

"Oh, you meant literally," Rex chuckled.

"In Halifax, I had a hunch that you would go home," Rex explained. "I managed to get a flight from Halifax to Chicago and went straight to your apartment. When I got there, I thought I heard you. I knocked then phoned but there was no answer. I used my keys to let myself in and that's when I knew you were in trouble. I stopped Ricky and called for an ambulance for you."

"But where is Ricky now? He's just going to find me again. He's going to come here and finish me!"

"Trust me. He's never going to bother you again."

"Do the police have him? Is he in jail? What am I going to do when he gets out? He's proven that he can find me. He has too many connections. I don't know where to hide."

"I mean it when I say that he is never going to bother you or anyone else ever again."

"The only way that could happen is if he's dead..." Lily paused. "Is Ricky dead?"

"Yes, Ricky's dead."

"But how? What happened?" Lily put her hands over her mouth. "Did you...?"

"I don't want to trouble you right now with this."

"I need to know. What happened? What did you do?"

"I came in and found him about to inject you with a syringe. I put my Karate into uses that I never thought I would. After I got him off you, he fought me. I instinctively fought back. I was angry and scared. I didn't even know if you were alive. All I knew is that I had to stop him. So I did."

"Are they going to arrest you?"

"I called Detective Reynolds after I called nine-one-one. He came right away and assessed the situation. I'm not being charged with anything. They are calling it self-defense."

Lily closed her eyes and laid her head back. She felt sore and tired. She recognized the sensation the pain killers gave her and she enjoyed it. She considered it a free high. She may have gotten clean, but she would always be an addict. She knew that she would have to eventually go through rehab again to come off the morphine she was being administered legally and freely in the hospital. She would cross that bridge when the time came. She drifted back to sleep.

"Lily," Rex's voice woke her. She opened her eyes, remembered that she couldn't see and closed them again. Instead, she lifted her hand and found his. She squeezed as a response.

"They're going to take you into surgery now. I'm going to be here when you wake up. Then I'm going to help you with your physical therapy. Together we will get through this."

"You once told me that you wanted to spend the rest of my days with me."

"I promised you that I would. I still want to."

"I once told you that I would never love you."

"I'll take whatever you have to give me."

"I'm going to have a long road ahead of me to recover from all of this."

"I'll walk every step of that road with you."

"I lied."

"About what?"

"About loving you. I've been in love with you for a long time. I was just so scared. I couldn't deal with it then and I still don't know if I can deal with it now. All I know is that I love you very much and I couldn't have gotten though any of this without you. I literally owe you my life. I don't want you to think that I love you out of gratitude or because I owe you. I really, truly do love you."

"Does that mean that you'll marry me?"

Lily smiled. "I'm not sure what the wedding pictures will look like, but have a priest standing by when I wake up."

Rex leaned over and kissed her gently on the mouth. Lily responded until the surgeon cleared his throat.

"If you guys are planning a wedding, we should get Miss Delphinium into surgery so we don't keep the poor groom waiting much longer," Dr. Powell said.

"I don't ever want to hear the name Dora again. That woman is gone. With your permission, I'd like to be Lily Rose Landers."

"I think that is the most beautiful name I've ever heard."

Lily smiled. "Me too. I'll see you in a few hours."

"I'll be here."

"I love you."

"I love you."

Lily was rolled away into surgery. Several hours later, Dr. Powell came to see Rex. He stood to greet the doctor. He couldn't read the expression on his face.

"How did it go?" Rex asked anxiously. "How is she?"

"She's one tough young lady," Dr. Powell answered.

"She's going to be alright?"

"Her eyesight should return to normal within a few weeks. Her speech may be a bit slurred and she may have some difficulties with her memory. There is some brain damage, but in time, it may heal itself. She needs a lot of rest, care and support. Her recovery may take years and it won't be easy, but from what I understand, she's going to have a lot of support."

"Can I see her?"

"Yes. She's still in recovery and starting to wake. I can only tell you to be patient with her, but the first thing she said when she started to regain consciousness is, 'Where's that priest?' I don't think she thought she was dying."

They all went to the recovery area to wait for Lily to wake up fully. Rex found a priest that humored them by allowing them to say their vows, knowing they would have to wait for the real ceremony. Until then, they considered themselves already happily married. It would be a long road, but with all that was behind them, they knew things could only get better and their relationship stronger and happier.

....

Threshold never played again as a group, but Rex and Mike continued to work as songwriters. Lily improved and eventually attended college to get her therapist degree and began working in the very rehab center that she had been a patient at. Pam became one of the top twenty most successful entrepreneurs in the United States. Peter found full time work and he and Cindy settled in Lily's old house, raising their young family. Cora continued to find her work as a nurse fulfilling and moved to a teaching hospital to help others become the best nurses they could be. Andy enjoyed his desk job and proved to be an excellent grandfather. Benjamin continued in his role as producer and promoter and soon was busy with other young bands starting out.

Rex and Lily not only shared their experiences, strengths, weaknesses and fears with each other, they went on to speak publicly about it. Lily stood in front of audiences once again. This time it was not to entertain, but to inform young people of the dangers of drugs and life on the streets. She was interviewed on many talk shows and was given a contract to write an autobiography. There was suggestions of a made for television movie as well.

To complete their life, Rex and Lily enjoyed life as parents. They had two very healthy and happy boys. Everything that Lily once felt eluded her future was a part of her life. She still had nightmares and very real fears, but those, too, were becoming less frequent. After years of therapy and counseling, she came to terms with her past and learned to move forward. She and Rex truly did share a pure and true love. They traveled separately down tragic paths, but they each lead to one they could travel down together. They only needed to find each other to begin that journey.

CPSIA information can be obtained at www.ICGtesting.com
Printed in the USA
LVOW082308070113

314726LV00001B/38/P